FINDING GRACE AND ELLIE

FINDING GRACE AND ELLIE

a novel

KEN A LOCKE

This is a work of fiction. Any resemblance to any person or place is entirely coincidental.

Chimenea Press
chimeneapress.com

979-8-9991709-3-4 (paperback)
979-8-9991709-4-1 (ebook)

To Angie, who always has a shining smile

when I ask her to 'read just one more thing'.

It's you at the chimenea fire

that I want to impress with a good story.

CONTENTS

Part 1

MAC'S FARM

CHAPTER ONE

Mac drove the gravel road into town like he always did around breakfast time, in his Ford pickup, elbow out the window, with Smokey riding shotgun. His brain had told his foot to brake and slow down before he realized there was something different. When he looked off the side of the low bridge, he saw a boat stuck on a fencepost that was standing in the middle of the river.

"That isn't normal," he muttered.

Smokey raised his head, looked at Mac, but laid it back down.

A steady winking reflection flashed up at Mac from the boat.

"What's a canoe doin' on this little river?" he said aloud.

He drove to the far side of the bridge, stopped the truck, shoved it into park, and stepped out.

"I'm goin', ma'am. That's why I stopped." Mac still spoke to his wife, even though she'd been gone seven years.

He sidestepped down the bank and stood on the shore. The whole river wasn't 20 feet across, and the barbed-wire fence that spanned it had mostly collapsed, though the hedge wood posts still stood.

That post was why the canoe sat crossways to the current, oscillating up and down.

A body lay slumped the middle of the canoe.

"Well, that ain't good."

Mac looked down once at his boots and jeans, grimaced, and stepped into the muddy water. It hadn't even reached his knees by the time he got to the end of the canoe, grabbed the rope, and started pulling it back to shore. He scuffled a few feet upstream to an otter slide he could use to pull the canoe, which slid easily, up and onto the bank.

As he jerked the rope to get the canoe all the way out of the water, the body—a teenaged girl—raised her head and looked right at him. He dropped the rope in surprise and the canoe started to slide back into the river.

"Help me," she said. Her voice was scratchy and low. She didn't scream or even speak loudly.

"I'm doin' just that, ma'am. Hang on a second and I'll get this stable. We can get up to the road and call for some help."

"Please no! Don't call anyone!"

As he finished settling the canoe on the wild grass along the creek, he stood up and looked at her.

"Why in the world don't you think you need help here?" he asked. Gently, though; to a spooked animal.

"Just. Could you help me out of here, please? I could use *your* help… just not a bunch of other people's."

Mac put his arm around her waist, carefully, and walked her up the bank and to the truck; a memory of a three-legged race at the fair flashed through his mind. She smelled bad. Sick with something, but also dirty hair and morning breath. He helped her climb into the cab, murmuring "move over" to Smokey and then "here's your seatbelt" to her. The girl's head slumped sideways against the window while Smokey laid his on her leg. She glanced down at the dog. Patted his head. Shut her eyes.

Mac reversed off the bridge until he got to a field entrance, turned around, and drove back to his farmhouse. He couldn't understand why she didn't want anyone else to know about her predicament; but, until she could explain better, he'd follow her wishes. He pulled around back of the house, like he usually did, putting the truck in the ruts under the hackberry, out of sight from the main road.

"You come on inside, now," he said, "we'll getcha settled and see what's what."

She nodded but still hadn't spoken since the creek. Mac slow-walked her into the front room and onto the divan. He'd taken the plastic off it a year or two ago, arguing with his wife's ghost all the while. He regretted taking it off now, since this girl was dirty and smelly and he didn't have one bit of knowledge about cleaning upholstery. Another problem for another day.

The girl laid her head on the embroidered pillow, her feet still on the floor. She didn't have shoes. Just dirty feet. He gently lifted them and put them on the divan. She fit easily, laid flat like that.

"Couldn't be much more than 5 feet tall, that one," he mused. "Would you like something to eat or drink?"

She didn't answer because she'd fallen asleep. Mac left her alone. He sat across the room, watching and thinking.

After a time, Mac got hungry enough—he never did get any breakfast from the aborted trip to the café—that he put link sausages in the cast iron, toasted some bread, sliced tomatoes, found cheese in the fridge. He made two plates and carried them to the coffee table in front of the divan. Tapped her on the shoulder. Nodded to the plate when she opened her eyes.

When she had eaten, the girl looked down at her feet, her dress; flicked her hair.

"Could I wash, please? Then I owe you an explanation," she said.

"Of course. Let me get the room set up for you."

He laid out a couple of his wife's dresses, plus her gardening slacks and a shirt, not sure. It didn't pang in his heart like he thought it would when he opened the dresser. He wondered at that, but not for long.

Mac showed her the bathroom, towels, soaps. He then busied himself outside for a good 15 minutes, checking the livestock in the pen near the barn and thinking about what he *had* planned before he found the girl and how he now needed to just be flexible.

He could see into the kitchen from the farmyard, and when he saw a shadow cross the window, he headed back inside. He found her putting the teapot on the stove, lighting the burner with a match. She didn't say anything when he came in, but looked at him questioningly.

"Mugs are up there in the cupboard to the right of the sink. Teabags are, uh, maybe in the pantry? With the curtain. I don't really drink tea, but I'm pretty sure my wife keeps some—kept some—around for visitors. Behind you," he motioned with his chin.

"Thank you," she said so softly he could barely hear her.

After she'd made a mug of tea—and offered him some, which he demurred—the girl set the mug on the table, stepped to a chair, pulled it back and sat down. He took the chair across the table from her, turning sideways so he could stretch his legs out. Steam coiled up towards the ceiling from the tea.

"My name is DD. I ended up in that canoe because I was trying to get away from my parents and the guy who ran our farm," she said, looking down at the table. "I tried and tried to get my parents to come with me, but I couldn't find them last night. That guy, Alaine, has been runnin' them since the moment he stepped onto our porch, back when I was a little kid."

"I can't imagine you floated very far. Not on that little creek." Mac scratched his seed cap off his head and laid it down on the table. The appliance-yellow flower pattern of the tablecloth clashed with the green of the cap. He moved the cap from the table to his knee, one leg crossed over the other.

"No, it was after midnight when I left. That canoe we only used to go out and catch carp and catfish sometimes, but we always had a person on the bank that pulled us back upriver after we floated down a little to the catfish holes. Last night I got stuck a time or two on something or other. Fences or dead trees. I pulled myself free and basically just floated. Didn't even paddle." DD dunked the teabag a few times, lifted it and wrapped the string around the spoon. Squeezed tea out of it and laid the spoon down.

"So, figure the current is three or four miles an hour," Mac calculated, "and I saw you at eight-ish this morning. Call it seven hours of drifting. You're no more than 20 miles, maybe 25, from your old place."

"That doesn't sound very far. Not when you say it like that. I'd hoped to be worlds away by now."

"Well, ain't you, though? I didn't know there was a farm upriver that had a couple living there with a guy who messed their lives up. And you'd think, the way I eat in town almost every meal, that I'd have heard of something funny goin' on up there." Mac had a puzzled look on his face. "I wonder why no one ever talked about you all?"

"Yeah, we didn't go into town hardly ever. I couldn't tell ya how to get there, if I'm honest."

Mac sat back in his chair, one leg flung sideways so his boot heel sat outside the table leg, the other crossed at the knee holding him steady. He rubbed his leg and grimaced.

"Your leg hurt?" she asked, with a hesitant smile.

"Well, I'll tell ya. This one hasn't been right since I took a hoof a few years ago. That cow was mighty pissed off I was askin' her to come into the barn to have her calf. She was determined to go way out in the pasture. Kicked me when I got too close. It flares up when I crawl around in rivers," he chuckled.

DD's face filled with pity and mirth and joy and sadness and gratitude all washing over it at once, changing like the shadows in a sun-shower. She put her hand palm-down on the table and extended it towards him. Not touching, but reaching out.

"Thanks for getting me. I was about done in down there."

Mac paused at the moment, recognizing her profound emotion. "Glad to do it," he said. "No other way to handle that, I guess."

"Could I ask you a few questions?" DD said after almost a full minute of silence.

"Of course."

"Number one, could I stay here a few days until I feel better and until I get my bearings?"

"Of course you can. I've got two other bedrooms and you can take your pick. My wife is gone, but she always kept a good supply of linens and stuff. I'm not too whippy at all that, but, if you don't mind helping me out, we'll get a bed made and the bathroom set up for you."

"The least I could do is to help you to help me," she smiled.

"Question two?" he said.

"Well, this one's tougher, for sure. Number two is…"

Her eyes filled with tears. She looked out the big front window. Wrapped her arms around herself.

She added, "This is a two-parter, I guess."

Mac Tillman just sat still. Kept his face open and squared his gaze on her face. Tried to radiate calm. Like when you don't want to startle a doe with her fawns walking by.

"I don't trust anyone," DD said. "I'm trusting you because you saved me. But if you try and call anyone who is in charge of anything, I'll be gone. Don't know where, and that's no threat—how could it be?—it's just the way it's gotta be."

She continued after a long pause, "I had twin babies. Those people back there took them and wouldn't tell me where they sent them off to. I finally left after I realized that was the only way I was gonna find them. Would you help me find them?"

Mac, even though he tried not to react, couldn't hide the alarm on his face.

"You're tellin' me you've got babies somewhere? That they won't tell you about?"

She looked at him, nodding her head.

He levered his legs under him and practically hopped to his feet, jumping back from the table.

"Don't we have to find them?" Mac shouted. "Ain't that the right thing to do? We gotta call the sheriff!"

"You don't need to *yell* at me, mister, I know it's all messed up," she said, starting to cry. "Not only were they gonna just 'move on' without talking about it anymore—'God has a Plan, and babies for you are not in it'—they were gonna make me get married to one of the boys there. And please, like I said, don't call anyone!"

"Wait! How old are you?" he demanded.

"Old enough to have babies. That is all that matters, isn't it?" she shot back.

"No! That is not all that matters!" he fumed.

She pushed herself up from the table, her face suffused with emotion. Took her mug to the sink and rinsed it out, throwing the teabag away in the trashcan under the sink. She turned back to Mac with a deep breath.

"I hope you'll forgive me, but I need to take a minute to myself. I know I've caused a passel of problems for you already, and you want answers, but—" she paused. "May I go out to the barn and just walk around a minute? I'd want you to just let me be; I think you could use a second to think on these things I've told you, too."

"You won't run off? Like you told me you might? I'm just worried about you, is all," he finished lamely.

"I won't run off. You've still saved me. You're my only shelter right now. And, if we both can calm back down, we'll figure out this thorny problem. I just need a minute."

He nodded vigorously. Motioned to the back screen door.

"By all means, DD. You're not a prisoner, ok? I'll go check the stock out near the shelterbelt. I'll be back in about 15 minutes?"

"That sounds just right. Thank you."

He walked out the door after she did, turning right for the trees instead of left towards the barn, the way she went.

When he came back after a quarter of an hour—all was well with the stock; at least the animals were under control—he saw her sitting on the stump set right next to the barn. She waved and smiled, so he changed his path to go sit next to her. She patted the stump then laid her hands in her lap.

"You've got some beautiful horse tack in there. Do you have horses?"

"No, not anymore. I couldn't bear to see my wife's mare miss her so badly, so I gave her to some friends who have kids who can ride and take care of her. My horse... well, that's another story for another day, I guess."

"We didn't have riding horses over there," she said. "Plowing horse is all. I didn't have to do any plowing; man's work, you know."

Mac looked at her, shaking his head but saying gently, full of compassion for her, "You've got one way of seeing the world, don't you?"

Barn swallows darted into and out of the door of the barn, right above their heads. Their chirping punctuated the rustling of the sunflowers and the pigweed in the breeze.

"What other way would I know? I barely left that place. They told me. *Alaine* told me—told *us*—there was one way of doing things, seeing things, believing things… And somehow my mama and father just didn't push back. They let him be the main parent."

"Why'd they do that?"

"No idea. All I know is that mama quit reading me books soon after he showed up. I learned to read and all that, but those picture books and books about people out in the real world? Locked up somewhere in one of the rooms I wasn't allowed in."

DD pantomimed shutting a door and locking it then throwing away the key.

"In your own house? Is that what you mean?" Mac asked.

"At first, it was just our house. But then they built a few sheds. Made them like cabins with water and insulation and stuff. I went in a few times. Mostly when he wanted to lecture me." DD made a face during this, like something bitter was on her lips.

"This may be too soon, and you may never want to answer this, but..." Mac paused. "Was he the father? Of your babies?" He finished the question in a whisper, embarrassed to ask.

Her head snapped up to look at him with alarm.

"Oh, no! He never did any of that stuff! He wouldn't even talk about it hardly. That's the one thing he left to my mother. Well, and to my 'other mother.' His wife or partner or whatever he called her."

"So... how did you come to have babies?"

Mac was uncomfortable asking; and he could tell she was almost as uncomfortable talking about it. Nevertheless, he wanted that piece of the puzzle revealed.

"Yeah... that was Trout. We loved each other. No one told us not to. And mama never did tell me all about prevention, so I got pregnant."

Mac leaned back against the red barn wood and looked up at the sky, interrupted by a barn swallow now and then. Tipped his chin towards the creek just visible in the distance.

"Trout, huh?"

She laughed. "A fish name, right? That's what I said to him the first time I met him! And guess what his brother's name was?"

15

Mac smiled. "Carp? Catfish? Gar?"

DD laughed and, for a brief moment, she was a girl again, unbowed by all this heavy stuff.

"His brother's name is Pike!"

Mac sat forward, smiling and chuckling like a rusty hinge, and decided this young mother deserved his best effort to gather the tattered pieces of her life back into one basket. It's what his Jules would have insisted on doing.

When the funny moment passed and they sobered again, the two stood up in the shade of the barn.

Mac motioned towards the creek, "Want to take a short walk down there? We could keep talking, for sure, but I'd show you my Jules' favorite thinking place. You might could use it."

DD smiled in response and started walking that way. The farm road was two ruts with grass growing down the center. They each took a rut, walking next to each other.

Mac still felt a little overwhelmed by the situation. "Boy, there sure is a lot of ground to cover, DD."

"I'd like to apologize first off. I had a reaction when you yelled," she put her hands up in front of her. "I didn't know I'd do that; but I'm maybe a little skittish right now."

"Understood, and no apology needed. I apologize for my reaction—I meant no harm to you. I think I was more mad at those adults than anything."

DD nodded her acceptance.

Mac added, "So. No police or sheriff. How about a doctor? I'm guessin' you haven't been checked over for a while?"

They'd reached the huge oak tree that overhung the road and most of the creek. It was cool and green and shady under there. A serenity with a timeless quality painted the edges of their moods, offering a balm to soothe them.

"I don't think I've ever been to a doctor. Alaine just said it was 'God's will' if I was fine or sick or had problems being pregnant. My parents would ask Art and Katy for help when I was little, but once Alaine took over, he insisted we'd all be fine." She lightly shrugged her shoulders. "Sounds pretty dumb when I just lay it out there like that, I guess."

"And, just to be clear, your parents didn't argue with him on that point?" Mac asked, a hint of incredulity underneath his patience.

DD looked over at him, face tilted up slightly since he was so much taller, and shook her head, mouth pressed together. "Nope. I feel like mama might have had it in her at some point, but by then, it was pretty much a power struggle that she had lost. There was no reason arguing, cuz both father and Alaine would just start spouting the same lines about being in charge and she wasn't. If that makes sense."

"That doesn't make sense at *all*, DD, but I see what you're saying. Did anyone ever ask you what you thought about any of that?" he said curiously, without heat.

"Heck, no!" She grimaced. "Sorry. That's almost a cuss word."

They'd reached the creek. Two chair-sized limestone rocks sat on either side of the farm track, half-in and half-out of the water. Mac motioned her to one and he parked himself on the other.

"Not to worry," he assured her. "I've been known to let a few even worse than that one fly now and then. Time that cow kicked me… shoulda heard *that* sermon I gave," he laughed. "These are my Jules' favorite rocks by the creek. I'd find her here in all kinds of weather. You'd think she was in charge of the water flow, by how much she sat here. It gave her a lot of peace those last days."

DD sat in silence, looking around at the scene. A canopy of oak, beech, and sycamore trees kept the sun from glaring. The shallow water, dappled with shade and sun, held water bugs on the surface, minnows just under, and crawdads along the silty bottom.

DD's face cleared, and she said, "In answer to your question: yes, I think if we could see a doctor that would be good. But you've got to promise me that it would stay confidential. Alaine will find out cuz he somehow always knows everything. Is that possible?"

Mac looked doubtful and said, "Well. We'd have to go into town and see him. He's been lookin' after me, and my wife before she passed, since we were both kids on other farms."

"I'm not going into any towns. Never mind."

"DD, that's the way it's done! Let me at least call him; ask him how to handle it?"

"Let me think about it. Let's go back to the house."

They walked the road, next to each other, neither of them talking. It was a short distance to Mac's farmhouse. Smokey lay on the porch, having waited for them, and slowly got up to meet them.

"It feels safe here, Mac," DD said quietly. "I am thankful for that. And for you. You've done more for me today than I have any right to expect."

DD walked over to the bed of iris and sage. Mac followed her. His wife had planted the flowers and herbs, and they needed no help to keep growing. The only reason those plants were all still alive. Bees buzzed around the blossoms on the sage and ants crawled on the buds of the iris. Though Mac and

DD's worlds were upended, lots of things continued unchanged.

"Yeah, I guess call him," DD said of the doctor. "At least ask if he could come out here."

"Will do."

CHAPTER TWO

"Mac, can I talk to you outside for a sec?" said Doc Harms, motioning with his chin.

Doc Harms had come out on the morning of the third day after Mac pulled DD from the creek. Doc Harms was standing in the living room of Mac's house, having just examined DD in the spare bedroom. DD hadn't come back out yet, but Mac could hear her moving around. Mac heard the toilet flush, the water run, then DD's steps in the hallway.

"Well, Doc, I'd normally say yes. That's what we did with Jules. But this one? She's—" Mac waved his hand back and forth, an uncertain look on his face.

"It's tricky stuff, Mac. I can't just say it all in front of her!" Doc Harms added heatedly.

"I think you have to, Doc. I'm no legal *anything* to her. She wanted some help and she wanted a promise of confidentiality. But it's her medical info, ain't it? Sure as heck isn't mine," Mac pushed back.

"Good point. Ok. Well. Then, I better ask her if she wants to hear it all with you or without you," Doc Harms said. "I've been in practice for a long time, but this is a new one on me. It's been years since I've had to think about teen privacy."

"Go right ahead," Mac said with satisfaction.

DD called out to them from the hallway, "I can hear you, you know. Just because I'm young, and probably a little lost, doesn't mean my ears don't work."

"Right," said Doc Harms. "Uh, DD, do you want Mac to—" He motioned to the porch, raised his eyebrows.

"I'd like him to stay, Doctor. Now, please, tell me what my condition is. All of it," DD ordered.

Mac swept his hands to the divan and to the chair, "Sit down, why don't we? No reason we gotta stand up for this."

After they sat, Mac and DD on the divan and Doc Harms across the coffee table from them in the chair, Doc Harms flipped the page back on his clipboard and began a recitation.

"Amazingly, you're basically in good health. You've got a slight temp, but that could be from what you told me about your, uh, breasts hurting. You told me you had babies and that you stopped nursing abruptly—could be a mild infection from that change. That pain should go away in a few days, after your milk dries up. It'll be unpleasant, but shouldn't be a medical danger. I can give you some meds for that."

"You brought meds with you?" Mac asked, doubtfully.

"No, I'd have to run back to the office and bring 'em back out."

DD motioned him to continue, impatient.

"Like I said, you dodged a bullet, several bullets, since you haven't had any vaccinations. We could take care of that when I come back."

She looked alarmed. Pressed her head back against the rail of the divan. Slowly shook her head no.

"No? Why not?" Doc Harms asked.

"I'm not even exactly sure what you mean by vaccinations and by meds. I know I told you, but we didn't do any doctor or hospital or medical stuff with the people. My whole experience is with the livestock. So, I've got to know more about those shots. I'm sorry, but it's just that—"

Mac and Doc Harms could tell she had more to say and waited patiently for her to go on.

"I've only ever learned that medicine is for the weak. The doubting makes us weak and we should depend on the Lord," she finally answered. "I see your faces and don't like that pity I see. Don't pity me! *Teach* me! And tell me why I need medicines and let me decide!"

DD had finished speaking in a rush. Her face had gotten red and her forehead creased as her voice had raised.

"It's a whole different world out here, isn't it, DD?" Mac said. "Take a breath. It's ok. Today is the day you get to start making choices instead of being told what's what. I promise you that."

Doc Harms didn't say anything, but nodded his head along with Mac.

"I don't know why you're here," Doc Harms reassured her, "or how you got here, or any of that. But my oath—my promise—is that I'll protect you and your information from everyone and everything. Just us three."

Mac took a second to look at DD then swung over to Doc Harms and said, "How about DD and I talk through it all and I give you a call? I could maybe drop by when I'm gettin' some dinner, anyway."

DD smiled at that, nodded in agreement. "Thank you, doctor. I mean that," she said. "I don't mean to be a 'new experience' for you, but I guess that's what I am. I hate to be a bother."

"It's my pleasure," he replied. "And it's for sure no bother; I look forward to hearing from you."

DD mostly slept the rest of that day. She took a bath in the evening, and then helped Mac make supper for them both. The next day, DD picked up a few of the books in the front room, paged through them, put them back down. She followed Mac out to see the animals. Smokey trailed along with her, staying on the ground rather than hopping into the truck when Mac opened the door. Mac chuckled and climbed in without Smokey.

The evening of the fourth day, DD asked if she could start helping out around the farm.

"I feel like a queen ordering servants around if I don't help," she admitted.

Mac laughed when he said, "Well, heck. You don't ask for much. Are you ready to talk about the doctor and the medicines?"

DD paused. Then said slowly, "Could we have dinner?"

"Sure. That would be fine."

"I'd like to talk about it while we eat. Or after, if that's the way you do things."

"I'm fine to do it either way. Jules would talk my ear off as soon as I sat down to the table for supper, and then she'd keep at it after," he smiled at the memory.

DD cooked a fine meal. Ham steaks, garden greens, mashed potatoes, pepper gravy, fresh iced tea.

"I guess you did all the cookin' at the farm?" Mac asked, impressed by the spread.

"Oh, no, not all of it. We all kind of pitched in. Mama, me, Rosie. Sometimes there were other women who didn't stay long who came in and helped."

"Who did all the shoppin'?" Mac asked, as if inquiring about a foreign country.

"The men went into town. Rosie went with them, but Alaine never let her go alone. Mama and daddy had a car that was old before I was born, and Alaine made them use that car for errands. It was just a ratty old car. Made a lot of noise when it started up. Mama told me that we'd take a trip in it someday, and I remember her muttering about whether it would actually drive still."

Mac pushed his plate away a few inches; learned behavior that indicated he was full. "Well, this is darned fine supper. Thank you."

"You're very welcome." She had a blush tint to her cheeks. Like it wasn't normal to be thanked. "I think I want to go ahead with the medicines the doctor talked about. He said I wouldn't get sick from the shots, and that lots of people got them, and school kids had to have them, and it would help protect me plus my babies if I couldn't ever get sick from those diseases."

"Yep, it's pretty normal. Well," he stopped. "Not that you aren't normal, DD! I just mean—"

"I understand. I'm not normal but I'm normal, right?" she smiled.

"It's your situation that isn't normal."

"Right. What do you think about the shots?" she asked with a hint of worry.

Mac pushed air through his lips, "Oh, I think you're safe. You'll be right as rain. I seem to remember one or two of 'em made me a little sore in the arm. Maybe felt a little run down for a day. But nothing major. I couldn't tell any difference. Not like a superpower or anything."

DD having made the decision, Mac told her he'd call Doc Harms in the morning. He took a second to show her where the phone numbers were, right by the rotary dial phone, for Doc Harms, the police, the fire station, and the hospital. The paper that the numbers were written on was crinkled and faded. Two of the numbers were in Mac's handwriting, and two were in a different hand.

"Is that Jules' handwriting?" DD asked quietly.

Mac sighed, "Yup, sure is. She knew I wasn't the best at gatherin' information under pressure, so she set the Doc and the hospital up for me. I added the other two, well, after she passed."

27

DD said, her voice still soft, "I'd hear more about your Jules someday, if you want. She sounds like a lovely person."

"Oh, she was. That's for sure." Mac blinked hard a couple of times and paused. "I can't talk about her right now, but I'll share that with you. More than you want to hear, probably," he half-smiled. His face had emotion in it, but his voice had stayed steady.

DD stood up from the table, took his and her plates to the sink and started washing. "Super power?" she asked, recalling Mac's comment about the vaccination. "What's that?"

She listened while Mac explained about superheroes and what their powers were and about comic books and some more about how maybe someday they could go to the library right there in town and get some of those books that people wrote—normal people—about superpowers. DD was like a sponge that soaked up every little scrap of moisture, and Mac went to sleep during those days more tired than he'd ever been.

Part 2

FOX FARM

CHAPTER THREE

DD's parents hadn't intended to be parents. They found each other at a Renaissance Festival in Wichita, he wearing a period-authentic tunic and belt with handmade ankle-high moccasins, she with a flowing skirt, peasant blouse and laurels woven into her hair. She had chosen a roasted ear of corn and he a turkey leg from the same vendor, who told them, one after another, that they only took cash. He had some. She did not. He paid for her and asked her if she'd like to go to the archery range together after they finished "breaking their fast." She smiled and said "yes, but only if you don't mind getting beat by a girl at arrows."

They spent a part of nearly every day together after that. They took long, slow drives in the country, wishing and talking. They spoke of gardening, weaving, candles, bees, soap, canning, goats, chickens, whole groves of trees and fields of native grass. Of course, they loved each other physically— their mutual casual rejection of parenting did not extend to the practice of lovemaking. And they didn't mean to be bohemian in a rural America kind of way; that happened naturally.

On one of their drives, they saw a farmhouse, set back from the road on a full quarter-section of land, that looked like it hadn't seen an owner in years.

Carly made an exuberant hand-painted sign from her art supplies that said *Will this owner kindly contact us? We want to RENT!* and tied the sign to the green gate with a leather cord. The sign included Mitchell's apartment address at the bottom; neither had a landline phone, and it was long before cell phones existed, for common people anyway. Their casual acceptance that "if it was meant to be, it will happen" extended to finding a way to live on that farmland. It didn't occur to either of them that they may have to make more of an effort past hanging a pasteboard sign.

Two weeks passed while Mitchell and Carly worked their food service jobs, having to wash french fry grease out of their hair and off their skin when they got done, before an envelope arrived. A shaky hand had copied out the address, the script angling up slightly. A grimy thumbprint sat under the return address. Mitchell opened it and read:

Hello. Your sign caught my attention as I drove by. My wife Katy and I own that place. But have no one left to live there. Our kids all moved away. You'd do me a favor by living there. Meet me at the farm after the noon meal on the first Sunday after you get this. We can make a deal. Sincerely, Art Gfeller.

"Woohoo! This is it, Carly!" Mitchell whooped.

"Ah! I can't believe it!" she hollered.

They danced around his tiny apartment long enough for the downstairs tenant to hit the floor with a broom. They collapsed onto his futon, laughing hysterically, joyfully taking each other's clothes off to celebrate.

The following Sunday, as directed, they sat in Mitchell's old Sentra by the closed gate. At 1:15, he saw a rooster tail of dust in the rear view, and nudged Carly.

The truck slowed and turned in at the gate. An old man stepped down from the truck. Tipped his cap at them, nodded towards the house, unlocked the gate, went back to his truck, and drove through right up to the porch. Mitchell drove up and parked next to the truck, nose-in.

"I'd letcha live here if you promise to take care of the property," the old man declared without introduction. "It needs a good clean. Well should still have water, but I haven't pulled the pump handle in a good five years, being honest. A lot of those trees in the shelterbelt are dead; maybe you'd plant some new ones if I brought 'em out?"

"Hell, yeah, we can do that," Mitchell smiled.

The old man looked at him, alarmed, then smoothed his face. "I'd appreciate a little less cursing, if you don't mind," he grimaced.

"Sorry," Carly chimed in. "We'd be glad to clean up and plant and look after and take care of this place."

The old man pushed his hat back, scratched his forehead. "How's 300 sound?"

Mitchell and Carly shared a wide-eyed glance and a quick nod to each other.

"Absolutely we can pay you 300 dollars a month!" Mitchell exclaimed.

The man squinted. Shook his head.

"That isn't what I meant," the man said. "Not at all. I meant I'd pay *you* 300. As caretakers, you see. Farmhands."

Carly flung her arms around Mitchell, then stepped to the old man and stretched her arms around him, too. He stood in surprise for a few seconds until he used both hands to pat her shoulders lightly. He cleared his throat as she stepped back.

"You won't regret this, mister!" Carly laughed. "I promise you that!"

"Oh, I can tell you two are the right ones for the place," he finally said with a grin. "Call me Art."

Carly and Mitchell moved in, made a new home, and busied themselves trying to do everything the old-time prairie settlers had done. They even tried to mimic some of the Native practices they read about.

Anything and everything to love like the world wasn't exhausting around them; an enclave against a societal cancer they wanted no part of.

CHAPTER FOUR

The "no-kids" thing, though. One winter, when the wind howled through the single-pane windows on the north side of the house, Carly sat straight up in the easy chair by the fire. Looked at the ceiling, counting on her fingers. She slumped back. Tapped her fingers on the armrest. Pursed her lips in and out for a minute or two. Then she got up to go find Mitchell.

As exultant as she was to feel the babies kicking (once she accepted the reality), her depression blackened and thickened when she quit feeling the movement. The books (from a trip into town and the thrift store; a birthing book only a few years outdated) said not to worry, a piece of advice she didn't—couldn't—follow. It also said to go to a doctor, just in case. She didn't follow that advice either.

"This is exactly why I didn't want kids," she screamed in Mitchell's face.

"I know, honey," he murmured.

They were both exhausted. She from laboring through the night. He from listening to her blame him for every one of those minutes.

The babies, when they came, were perfect in every way except one. Both tiny bodies had finally slid from her body, blue-ish, with the birth cords still pulsing slightly. Mitchell clumsily cut the cords, massaged the babies, just like the book said. Just like the prairie wisdom magazine *said* would work. When Carly didn't hear crying, she sat forward and grabbed one of them herself, massaging then patting then pounding on its back.

No color came to either child. Both of them stillbirths, perfect in every single detail. Except the most important one—a heartbeat.

Carly moaned and Mitchell moaned with her.

"Let's name this one Doug. Let's name this one David," she eventually rasped, her throat raw from crying.

The closeness of the room had sickened her in a rush; the still air full of bodily smells, the sheets all wet from sweat and birthing water plus a little blood. She walked outside as soon as she could get up from the wet bed sheets, when Mitchell had just looked at her, from between her legs, with a broken face she hoped never to have to see again. The bodies of her two perfect (almost perfect) boys lay next to each other, still touching like they had in the womb, at the foot of the bed. They had a whiteness to them that seemed alien; although Carly hadn't seen any other babies, she was pretty sure a beating heart would have given them the color she expected. And the hope she desperately needed.

Carly screamed into the row of trees outside. From deep within her. The force of the scream delivered the afterbirth, which slipped out of her with only a hint of resistance. She barely registered it leaving, so detached was she from the horror of the moment.

She'd pinned her depression to this point in time, saying, almost as a mantra:

It'll all be better when the babies are born.

Mitchell will be gentler with me when the babies are born.

Mitchell will stop yelling at me when the babies are born.

Mitchell will stop slapping me when the babies are born.

I won't get nauseous at the smell of tomato soup when the babies are born.

I won't have to shovel pig poop when the babies are born.

The looming reality of abuse was almost entirely in her own head; Mitchell might have been dismissive and a little self-absorbed, but, in her opinion, he had never trended towards abuse of any variety. Still, her mind filled itself without permission or forgiveness and she was powerless to control any of the thoughts.

Had she thought to consult another person, she would have learned that navigating Mitchell's temper was not only exhausting, but also a flag of warning.

She finally turned to go back inside when her shivering body awoke her to reality, and insisted she seek heat. And maybe a washrag.

"I'm so sorry, Carly," Mitchell said. It was the most tender he'd been since she'd gotten pregnant.

She looked at him, stopped just inside the door. "I've failed us. I'm the one who should be sorry."

"You did everything right, Carly. We'll try again."

He stepped toward her, but she held her hand up. He stopped. They both wept. They both needed to wash. He from the sweat of fear and the ever-present funk of animals, she from the exertion of child-bearing, the coppery smell of blood.

"I want to wash the babes," she said.

"Oh, Carly… are you sure?"

She sat on the couch. Looked down. She sat motionless for so long that Mitchell had started to reach out to shake her, in case she was dying, too.

"No. But it's the only thing that makes even a tiny bit of sense to me right this second."

He followed her into the bedroom, where she collapsed to her knees at the sight. The bodies had turned into an alabaster carving. The slick wetness had dried on them in a film, a mockery of the caul that was supposed to portend health and wellness and good fortune. She paid no heed to any of that and knelt at the foot of the bed, wrapping one arm each around each child, her head between them, hair fanned by the speed at which she flung her head down.

Sobbing. Deep from within her. Deep enough for her to feel like the connective tissue that held her organs in place, her heart in its place, had shredded and her organs were collapsing into a primal jelly. The only thing that remained was sadness and despair. She had no way of knowing those feelings would never truly leave.

Mitchell could only stand at the door and watch. He had nothing to offer her but another chance, and even as dim as he was about intuition, he knew this was not a good time to initiate sex—to try again. His heavy ranch coat hung on his shoulders; it had been tight on him when he bought it, before they'd worked through summer, fall, and early winter. He had reduced himself to a scarecrow. His cheekbones stuck gauntly out from his face, and his beard could no longer camouflage his weight loss. The smell of the pig shit on his boots rose up past his face and burrowed into his beard and hair. From that day on, he'd always associate the smell of hogs with this awful day; wishing it gone as soon as the memory started playing.

"Bring the tub from the kitchen, please," Carly said. "Warm some water, too. Please."

"I'll do that."

Mitchell turned for the kitchen, shrugging out of his coat as he went down the hallway. He hung it on his chair at the table. He grabbed the big galvanized tub off the hook on the wall, pushed it under the faucet, began filling it. When it was halfway, he turned the water off, balanced the tub on the lip of the sink, and lifted it with the handles. It was too wide to carry down the hallway, so he half-turned and half-twisted it with his arms to get to the bedroom. He set it down next to Carly, who was still sobbing. She put her hand down, checking the water.

"Warm water. Did I not ask for warm water?" she snapped.

"Carly. The water temperature doesn't matter to them."

She rose in a fury, turned on him.

"If you think for one second that I'm going to wash my poor dead babes in cold water just so you can save some effort lighting a fire to *warm some water* then you are sadly mistaken!"

"It's just that—"

"Do what I say, *for once*, without telling me why your way is better! I want some warm water and I want it *now*."

Her voice had lowered into a hiss at the end; he had never heard that from her before.

"I'm sorry. You're right. I'll go heat some water."

She looked at him then, watching his hands to see if he meant his words, or if he was using them as decoys to a coming beating. He turned on his bootheel and left the room. She soon heard a match striking and the clank of the heavy stockpot being filled with water and put on the stove.

When he came back, he carried the stockpot with near-boiling water, which he dumped into the washtub. She checked the water, nodded once.

"Thank you, Mitchell. It's just right," she said, looking at him.

He dipped his chin, held her gaze.

Both faces softened. Though Mitchell would have been shocked that Carly thought a beating was coming, or even harsh words were coming, it was still a moment of importance. A crisis passed, apologies accepted, and they both reached to lift the tiny babe they'd named Doug and put him in the water. Carly was careful to keep Doug's face out of the water as she gently spooned it over him with her hand. Mitchell held the child's feet and kept him under the surface, using his other hand to gently stroke the impossibly soft skin and wipe the remains of the caul away. Carly slicked the babe's sparse hair back as she washed his head. Both of them wept steadily as they washed, though neither of them made a sound.

David's washing was much the same. He had a great deal more hair, and he had a rough patch of skin on his left shoulder that somehow looked red and chapped. Carly petted it, committing the roughness to memory, before she moved on. Mitchell marveled at the tiny toenails, thinking of how he trimmed the nails of the baby goats. Wishing he could breathe life back into these two so he could watch their nails grow.

They wrapped each separately, then together next to one another, in a series of sheets and towels. Carly and Mitchell rose together, sharing the bundle, and walked outside. After Mitchell got a shovel, they kept walking, through the young trees they'd planted, across the small pasture, all the way to the grand cottonwood at the edge of the river. Mitchell started digging and went on until he had struck a network of roots from the tree. He found a gap in the roots and dug another foot down. The dirt had turned muddy and sandy. He looked at Carly, who nodded.

She stepped into the hole, balanced on two roots so her bare feet stayed dry, but more so the burial place would not be sullied, and together they placed

Doug and David right down there, together forever, in the roots of the sentinel cottonwood, now with two new guardians. Mitchell stepped out, pulled Carly back up, and wordlessly refilled the hole. A small mound of dirt rose a few inches above the grasses and he placed the patch of turf on top of it, stepping on it to seal the patch to the dirt. To close the tomb.

Mitchell dragged the shovel behind him as he trailed Carly back to the farmhouse. No birds sang.

It was a new moon, which should have been a good sign. Instead, it made the walk back all the darker, and dawn was far away.

CHAPTER FIVE

Mitchell and Carly eventually conceived another child. They survived a very dark winter, an ebullient spring that mocked their despair, a scorching summer that seared the fury of their loss into them like a wood-burning tool, and, finally, an easing of the heat into an autumn of promise. This time the due date was solidly in the late spring. "No more cold, dark winter labor pains, Mitchell," she'd said with a soft smile. He returned that smile with a caress of her cheeks and a low "I love you, Carly."

They took care of each other better this time. Mitchell's tendency to paint his temper on or at Carly had subsided. He cared for her with a tenderness that was like their first days, rather than at their lowest right before the tragedy of the twins. He learned how to cook more than just soup from raw vegetables, and she showed him how to work most of the kitchen machines. They shared the chores: paying the bills (electricity was cheap, but the rural co-op still needed some money), caring for the (lots of) chickens and (just a few) cattle plus the pigs. They'd found various farmers and ranchers through Art who would drop off feed or silage. Mitchell would take the old Sentra over and help those same guys now and then in exchange for the products. Art faithfully paid them 300 dollars a month and that went to pay for the things that Mitchell and Carly didn't produce or make or mill or harvest themselves.

When you don't need to dress to impress, a family can live pretty cheaply out in the farm country of the middle of the Great Plains a few miles from anywhere.

"Mitchell," she yelled one afternoon.

"I'm here, Carly!"

"It's time. And I just felt a kick before this contraction."

"This is gonna be a piece of cake, Carly."

His grin stopped just short of frantic, but she could see the wild in his eyes itching to get out and run across the fields. Her soul saw that and clamored to go with him. Escape all this biological necessity and just run. Maybe even so fast that she would lift above the bluegrass and soar like the red-tail hawks they watched.

Hours later, her final push delivered the afterbirth that Mitchell wrapped in a pillowcase. Set on the floor to deal with in a minute. He'd put a tiny, perfect, breathing girl into Carly's arms a few minutes ago. They both leaked tears while Carly cooed to her. They couldn't stop looking at how perfect she was.

Mitchell went to the kitchen to get the small washtub, filled it with a mix of cold tap and boiling water to just the right temperature. He had a bad moment when he turned his shoulders sideways to get the tub through the doorway remembering the twins, but he gave his head a shake—like a horse flicking a horsefly away—and set the tub next to the bed with a look of love and assurance.

"Warm water, Carly. When and if you want to give her a bath."

"Let's do that, Mitchell. I'd like to put this gown on her before we say her name out loud."

They took turns using the soaked felt cloth on the babe. She had enough hair that they could see a part on the left side of her head that started with a swirl near her forehead. By the time they'd finished the bath and put her in the gown, she was grizzling and moving her head around. Carly put the baby's mouth near her breast and watched in amazement as the baby began to nurse. Mitchell sat on the bed, in cleaner clothes this time, and wept at the beauty.

"Finally," he murmured.

"What's that?"

"She's our payoff, Carly. All that... before. Up 'til now. Here's the payoff."

In Carly's grief, back when the twins died, she promised the next baby's life to God, if only He would let it live. This day, in a sigh of fealty, she gave this child one name from each dead twin.

"I'm not sure if you remember me saying this, Mitchell, when we buried our boys. But I'd like to name her for them. Doug David. Can we?"

He sat for a minute, rubbed his chin. The whiskers rasped against his callused hands.

"I wondered if you'd stick to that. And, of course, we can."

She smiled in response. Closed her eyes. Suddenly weary from the birthing and the nursing. Thirsty.

"Could you get me some cold water, please?" she asked.

"On my way, hon."

While he walked down the hallway, Mitchell thought about the delivery of the stillborn twins. His unspoken promise that he would do anything—*anything*—to avoid having to see that look on her face again. That broken-glass, choking fear and despondency she'd sunk into. He was pretty certain it was going to be a burden and a trial to lay dead brothers' names on a newborn, but he'd be damned if he was the one that was gonna point it out to anyone.

As she listened to Mitchell walk away, and as she nursed her baby, Carly realized that the heavy cloak of blackness had lifted from her chest. She knew by now that depression flitted at the corners of her spirit like a blackbird on a wire. She hoped it would stay away now that she had the baby to care for. The litany from

48

before had coalesced into *My life will be perfect once this baby is born.* Simple, eternally hopeful, hopelessly overbalanced. No one can carry that burden of expectation, especially not a new mother and child. A tiny voice said it was stupid and wrong and selfish to make her perfect infant daughter tote around two dead names. It would take only the briefest pause of doubt in her mind and a nod towards the insistent voice for that truth to root, bloom, and produce fruit. Carly both knew it and ignored it, almost without any time passing at all.

She looked down at her daughter, "DD it is, little one. You've got it all now. The good *and* the bad."

CHAPTER SIX

When Doug David was only two, Carly had first taken her out to the cottonwood. Carly loved the similarity of DD's blonde hair and her own auburn hair that flowed in straight sheafs down their backs like waterfalls. Mitchell cut Carly's twice a year right at the middle of her shoulder blades. Carly kept Doug David's hair the same way, although the blonde shade reflected sunlight like joy just as easily as it absorbed the foggy days; those dark days when Carly's spirit was awash in grief for her first two boys.

Carly hadn't told her yet why she had two boy names. On the worst of the dark days Carly clung to Doug David like driftwood in a whirlpool. When they sat on the roots of the cottonwood close to the trunk, perched on the wide bark right above the sandy soil, Carly simply held Doug David's hand. Carly had learned that the easiest way through the sadness about the boys was to let the wave hit her, immerse her, then wait for it to drain away rather than try to keep her spirit above it all. This could take an hour, or a day, or sometimes days on end. Doug David sat close, knowing her mother needed her, even if she didn't understand what was at stake.

The presence of her daughter operated as an anchor. Not one that dragged her to the bottom of the depressive wave, but one that stopped her from being dragged along underwater—kept her pointed into the waves so she didn't swamp sideways—an anchor that held Carly to a place where she knew, at least some of the time, that her head would be above the tide. Hydrodynamic theory aside, she clung to the belief that Doug David could be a talisman during those times when she mourned the two almost-perfect babies. Carly would survive as long as Doug David did.

Mitchell had tired of her talking about it. He had exhausted all his well-meaning words and encouragement several years ago. In his world, nothing would change the grim reality of their loss, and talking about it just kept the sad thoughts in the churn, when he really just wanted it all to sink to the bottom and never be heard from again.

Most days it was enough that he could enjoy DD. They walked the property all the way to the river and then over to the cedars and then to the fence where they could see the road. DD laughed at butterflies, at cow poop, at the chickens squawking as they ran first towards them and then away. She stood quietly looking at the water swirl past in the creek, holding her daddy's hand. He'd sometimes point out the fish jumping or the turtles sunning themselves. The canoe stayed pulled up on the bank; he was too scared to get in it with her, not being a strong swimmer himself. He promised her that someday he'd take her out in the boat and they could paddle up and down until they got bored with it.

After Mitchell had been gone overnight, helping one of the farmers out with the wheat harvest, he came home with a huge grin on his face. He parked the car askew in the front yard, tooted the horn, once and then again, until both Carly and DD were standing on the porch. Grinning themselves cuz they were happy to see him. He hollered out the window.

"Come on out here!"

"You come up here!" DD said back.

"Come on! It'll be worth it, I promise," he yelled.

He laughed and smiled again at them and got out. He went to the back door of the car, waited until DD got there to open it.

Out spilled a little golden retriever mix puppy, paws all huge and tongue wagging. DD fell to her knees and tried to pick up the puppy, who went boneless and wriggled back down to the ground. The puppy jumped and yipped and licked and dashed to and away from DD. Carly put her arms around Mitchell and laid her head on his shoulder.

"Well?" Mitchell asked, "Whaddya gonna call him?"

"Are we keeping him, daddy?" DD squealed.

"You're keeping him, DD! And you get to name him and feed him and sleep with him and tuck him in at night and everything!"

At that, Carly looked up at him with alarm, mouthing *sleep with her?* but not loud enough for DD to hear.

"It makes me so happy! Thank you, daddy! I'm gonna skip!"

She did just that—one lap around the car and then one lap around her mom and dad. The puppy followed her.

"He loves skipping," she said, already an authority. "I'm gonna call him Skip."

"Skip, huh?" Mitchell asked, amused. "Not Skipper or Skippy?"

"No way. Those names aren't right. He's Skip," she insisted. "Aren't you, Skip?"

CHAPTER SEVEN

Six years later, Doug David continued to find joy on the farm. Her shining blonde hair flew behind her as a flag of happiness, if there was such a thing. Her joy gave her face a lightness, a brightness that both absorbed and reflected the sun. She ran to her mother with a fistful of flowers in one hand and a stick in the other. She'd stop now and then to throw the stick for her dog to fetch, though the dog tumbled to a stop at her feet when she stopped, and only panted when she repeated the word "fetch" six or seven times. DD would laugh then, and pick up the stick and run back in the general direction of the house. Skip had stayed a small dog, more a beagle size, even though he looked just like a golden retriever.

"Hello, mama!" she cried.

"Well, if it isn't my favorite daughter!" Carly laughed as she straightened from pulling weeds in her flowerbed.

"I'm your *only* daughter, mama," the girl smiled.

"I know that, my sweet. What have you been doing?"

"I went to the river. Just to *look* at the river, not to *touch* it," she assured her mother.

"Yes. Thank you for remembering the rule. How was it today?"

"Good. I sat under the tree. At the place you say is your favorite in the whole wide world."

"Oh, that's so sweet, Doug David. I do love that place," Carly said, running her hand along her daughter's hair.

"Can we eat? I'm hungry!"

"Of course, little one. Come on in."

DD's parents cared for her with a fierce and glee-filled love. Mitchell showed her worms, beaver dams, fishing, almost sooner than she could walk. Carly taught her baking and cooking, caring for the small farm animals, sewing, even some painting. The family of three existed in a cone of exclusion, Art Gfeller happy to check on them weekly to bring them last week's requested goods, and take the list for next week. They gave him a portion of the farm's produce, both plant and animal, which satisfied Gfeller—never a bottom-line guy—who was still just happy to have the property cared for.

After DD had eaten her fill of cheese and crackers, Mitchell's face brightened and he put a finger up in the air.

"DD, come on and let's take the canoe over there and see if we can see some baby frogs!" Mitchell said.

"Oh, daddy, can we? I bet we find a ton and we can bring some home to show mama!"

"Put this orange jacket on first. Just in case we tip. It'll help ya float."

"Float? You mean we are gonna get wet?" she said with alarm.

Carly interrupted, "Hey, now you two be careful! You know she's pretty special, right, daddy?"

Mitchell laughed and nodded at Carly with a smile. To DD, he said, "Nope, not unless the canoe tips all the way over. I won't let that happen. But, still, ya gotta be careful when you get in this canoe and go on the river. You never know."

"Yeah, but if I'm always with you, you'll save me, won't you?"

"Doggone right I will. Nothin' to worry about," he laughed.

"So why do I have ta wear this, then? It sticks out and makes my neck feel all squished."

"Well, now, DD, just leave it on. See that belt thing there? Just swing it around your back and snap it in the front. Better safe than sorry."

"Just like being around the cows?"

"Yep, exactly," he smiled. "Ready?"

He launched the canoe down the bank with DD in front while he took one giant step in the water and then sat down in the seat at the rear. He used his river leg to push off and point them towards the far bank, barely three canoe lengths across.

"It's not a mighty river, is it, DD? The Ninnescah is little but important. Carries water all over the state and down into the next one. See where the sand is here?"

"Yep, I see it," she said, hanging on to the sides of the canoe.

"That's sand that's all been dropped there by the river. This is kind of a bend in the river, so the water goes slower here on this far side. The inside of the curve. So anything floating along gets dropped off. Anything that goes along the outside stays in the water and goes downstream."

"Daddy, that's boring talk. Where are the frogs?"

Mitchell laughed with her and paddled the canoe so it slid up onto the sandbar and stuck fast. He stepped out and pulled the canoe up even farther so it wouldn't float away.

"Come here," he said, holding his hand out to her. "Over on the other side of the sand is a small pool. Look in there and see if there's anything swimming around."

Sure enough, like a tide pool, there was moss, reeds, bubbles, minnows, and tadpoles.

"I don't see any frogs, daddy," she said.

"See those swim things? Those are called tadpoles, and if we let them grow another week or two, they turn into frogs. Wanna take some home to mama?"

"You bet I do!"

Mitchell handed her a mason jar and a homemade net: cloth stretched between a stick shaped like a "Y."

"Catch a bunch—they'll be fine on the way back. We can put them in the pond that we get water out of for the chickens and the pigs."

DD splashed happily around, getting both of them wet, before she got the hang of the net and caught half a dozen tadpoles, plus some bonus minnows, to put in the jar.

"Seem like enough?" Mitchell asked.

"Yup. Let's go put them in the pond."

"Here. Put this lid on the jar, not too tight. Don't spill it over or slosh it too much. They won't like that."

"We better name them, huh, daddy?"

"You bet!"

When they got back to the farm-side bank, he'd stowed the canoe, and they got close to the farmhouse,

DD started yelling for her mama. Carly dashed out the back door, looking worried.

"Guess what we got, mama?"

"Are you both ok?"

"Oh, sure, mama—we got," she paused, and looked at her dad, "what are they again?"

"Tadpoles," he whispered.

"Tadpoles!" she exclaimed with glee. "They turn into frogs! They're goin' in the pond!"

CHAPTER EIGHT

In those days, Doug David lived in an idyllic cheerfulness. And why wouldn't it feel that way? There had been no bad thing to mar her happiness. Not even her perfect little puppy had suffered so much as a cold, and somehow, against the odds of the myriad medical problems in existence, they all stayed healthy and hale. Although some of the great figures of history had been undone by the most prosaic of maladies, sickness had avoided the Foxes to this point. The farm property had turned out to be a closed environment of sorts; a terrarium. Mitchell and Carly had lived through school inoculations like other kids of the late 20th century, but they didn't think they needed to subject Doug David to the same humiliations. Their plan, after all, was to stay there forever and ignore the degradation of the world outside.

That ever-present equalizer, money, showed its force now and then. A few times a year they needed things that Art's stipend didn't cover or they just couldn't barter for. Mitchell thought about hiring himself out to work, reluctantly, but tried to take advantage of Carly's talents first. It wasn't like his life was so stuffed with effort, while taking care of the farm, that he didn't have some free time every day.

Mitchell had gotten used to having a lot of free brain space while he worked, though, and the thought that he'd have to go take orders from someone, anyone, put him in a bad mood. Carly watched him carefully still for those bad moods. His forehead creased when he carried internal anger, and his eye sockets deepened and shadowed. Carly walked carefully around him when he looked that way, like most souls who have to dance around a partner who considered their own needs higher than a family's security. He hadn't hit her since the twins—*Had he ever, really?* she wondered—and had only raised his voice a few times. Mostly when DD was irritable and Carly took DD's side; Mitchell felt ganged up on those times. Carly was quick to remove DD from the situation. Defusing was the quickest and safest way through.

"Carly, you could sell some of these paintings, ya know?" Mitchell said now and then, deferring decision on taking his own outside work initiative.

Carly hid a moment of doubt from them both. She didn't think it was helpful to show vulnerability about her value to the art world. Thought it was weak. Thought it would be a bad example for DD. It stemmed from both her dead twins and the ensuing postpartum depression and her failure to get pregnant again after DD. Dual thoughts battled in Carly when Mitchell said stuff like that. *Why doesn't he get off his own ass and find work? It's not like he couldn't.*

Why do I have to be the one who solves everything around here? Sometimes I wish a leader would show up—just tell us what to do. Carly was careful not to verbalize any of that, of course, because it would push Mitchell's eyes deeper into their sockets, and the shadow would act like a cloak of darkness putting weight on all three of them. Her ability to stop her spiral into depression waned as this pattern repeated itself. It got harder and harder to hide from DD, which took more energy—that manic glee she used to cover the imbalance—and from Mitchell, who had started to watch her. Not look at her. Not admire her. But to watch her, like a guard waiting for the rebellion.

She settled on replying, "Mitchell, you know that would mean trying to start that old car of yours or getting a ride from Art, packing the paintings, *meeting people,* and making small talk. No thank you!" she laughed, stifling the manic yelp at the back of her throat.

"Well, still, you've got a talent, and that's for sure." His face softened. A good moment.

"And you're an expert?" she chuckled.

"I love them too, mama!" Doug David said.

They all looked at each other fondly, knowing they didn't need to leave, didn't want to leave; they had everything they could wish for right on this very farm.

The dichotomy of trust and distrust existed among them as weeds among the flowers. It just *was.* Talking about it didn't occur to either Carly or Mitchell as a good idea or even a strategy to stay close. It was enough to have their wish, imperfect or not. They similarly avoided the discussion that another child or two, or even a bunch, would make them happier. Another baby hadn't happened for them, out there all alone on the Fox farm, and they didn't question it.

On a typical evening, Carly said to DD, "I've got to get these carrots and potatoes cooking. Will you take these peelings and throw them over the fence to the chickens for me? Then come right back in and get the last of them, ok?"

"Sure, mama." DD concentrated on putting all the peels onto a large flat metal plate. She was careful to pick up the ones that had fallen wide of the plate and put them on the top of the pile. She turned for the back door, nudged it open with her knee, and walked to the chicken coop.

One of DD's jobs was to come collect the eggs every morning, so she was used to the clucking and the rush of birds towards the coop. She was just tall enough to lift the plate above her head and tip the peels over the fence, which was much quicker than setting the plate down, opening the gate while shooing the chickens back, picking up the plate, going in, shutting the gate, then giving them whatever food she'd brought.

In the morning, she had no choice but to go into the coop and then the roost. There was no other way to get the eggs. Her papa always said he should've built the roost with a door on the outside so a person could just reach in and get the eggs, but he never changed the design. When she complained about it, he'd always say, "It's good for them to be used to a person walking among them anyway, Doug David." It took until DD was a few years older to realize that her father avoided that coop re-design out of laziness or maybe even spite—to make DD work harder than she needed to—rather than a zeal to train poultry.

She hated most getting the chicken poop on her shoes. DD only had three pairs, and the sparkly ones, which her mom had gotten from a catalog, were her favorites. She wore them once to get eggs, and had tracked poop all through the house before her mother noticed and rushed her outside to clean her shoes off. Her dad helped her, and he used a wire brush, knocking some of the sparkles off, which made her sad. "No other way to clean them, sweetie," he'd said. "Don't wear good stuff when you're doing farm work, remember? It's a tough lesson, but maybe this will help you think of it."

She didn't think she needed to learn a lesson about shoe-wearing, just because she was trying to make the best of the chores she did with her fancy shoes.

CHAPTER NINE

The first time Doug David had a fever, it scared both parents. Scared them enough to get the old car started up and drive to see the Gfellers, who were really the only people Mitchell and Carly knew out there. Mitchell carried Doug David, wrapped in a blanket, a damp washcloth on her forehead. They'd waited until sunset to go over. It was one of the first hot days of spring, and Doug David was five years old. They'd parked the car and barely stepped onto the concrete pad at the front door under the small stoop's roof before Katy Gfeller opened both doors wide to let them in.

"My word, what's gone wrong here?" she said. "You all come in. Lay her right down on the divan there."

Mitchell and Carly scurried quickly in and did as they were told.

"She's just so hot! She's burning up; we've tried everything," Carly said.

Katy fired off a barrage of questions. "Has she kept fluids down? Has she been on the toilet a lot? Can she eat? Did either of you two have these same symptoms?"

"She hasn't really been awake all day," Carly said. "Yesterday was a bad one, for sure, but she's quit from both ends, mostly. No, we've been fine. Which makes it all the more scary!"

"Well, she's dehydrated, for sure," Katy observed. "If we can't get some fluids down her soon, we'll need to take her on into town and get some medical help. It's not the end of the world to ask for help. Like you did just now." She smiled at them, to take the sting of fear away from the words "into town."

"We don't have money for a hospital," Mitchell said, squeezing his hands together. "I sure hope you can help us fix her up."

"Well, let's put some hot water on first, then let's get her in a bath," Katy advised.

She proceeded to bustle around for the next few minutes, making hot tea and broth. Katy's attention to Doug David's illness was a clinic in old-timer home remedies. She threw all her knowledge into the sickness and hoped some of it would stick. Carly didn't even have a thermometer. Katy produced an old one filled with mercury in a thick glass tube, gradations on a paper inside the tube. The numbers went from 97 to 106, and there was a bulb at the bottom filled with the silvery liquid.

"You guys remember this old type of thermometer? Standard with every farmhouse, I say," Katy laughed.

"Let's try it out. Just prop that under her tongue and keep her mouth closed. It takes a while."

Doug David lolled, still on what Katy had called a divan. Carly felt like she'd traveled back in time to her grandmother's house. A warmth that her own farmhouse lacked; she'd have to try and pin down what was missing. The curious incense of homemade bread and woodsmoke, with hints of earth and steam, were part of her nostalgia, for sure.

After a few minutes, Katy withdrew the thermometer from Doug David's mouth. "Well, her temp seems to stop at 104, which is really good news. Let's get her into the bath," she said, motioning for Carly to pick up her daughter. Katy added to Mitchell, "Would you mind going on out to the far shelterbelt and tell Art to come in for supper? He'll want to come in anyway, since it's getting dark. And he'll listen better if you tell him than if I do."

Mitchell headed for the front door, stepping back outside and turning for the trees. He heard a chainsaw in the distance and walked that way.

"Sometimes men sit and fret and make everything a little worse, if you want the truth," Katy said, after Mitchell had left. "She'll be fine, don't you worry. I've seen kids go through way higher temps and be just fine the next day."

They worked together to get Doug David's clothes off and then they slipped her into the bath. It was cool water, with Epsom salts in it, and they made a paste of baking soda that Katy said they should put on the girl's upper chest and forehead. "Be careful it doesn't get in her eyes, is all," Katie cautioned.

Carly daubed the paste on like she was making fine pottery, smoothing the edges of it and covering DD's forehead evenly left and right of the centerline of her nose. She had a shudder of memory about bathing her first boys. That warm water. Smoothing back their hair. The rough patch of skin on David's shoulder.

"Now," Katy said. "Let's see if we can get her to sip on this tea. It's cooled enough."

They held a China teacup of dandelion and some other roots brewed into a tea. Carly held Doug David's head up and put the cup to her lips, tipping it ever so slightly so her lips were wet. Instinct took over and Doug David opened her mouth, allowing Carly to pour a few sips in. She repeated this until the cup was empty.

Carly laid Doug David back against the curve of the porcelain tub, holding her in place so she wouldn't slip beneath the water. Her blonde hair needed a wash. It didn't shine like usual; just clung to her head in damp and greasy strings. The ends sat in the water, turning to a light, muddy brown with the wetness. She didn't look good at all.

"Is she getting worse?" Carly fretted to Katy. "Maybe we should take her to town?"

"Let's give it another half hour. We'll know by then."

In the meantime, Mitchell had found Art. He was sawing through some blown-down old trees, cutting them into manageable lengths that he could throw into the back of the pickup he had parked at the edge of the trees.

"Well, hello, there, Mitchell! I'm surprised to see you over here," Art said, after he turned off the chainsaw.

"Hello, Art. Katy sent me out to get you; said you'd be about done anyway."

"That's true. What brings you over in the first place?"

"Our Doug David is sick. She was burning up with fever and we didn't know what to do."

"Ah. Yeah, that's scary when the kids take sick. Well, I'll tell you what: there's no better nurse out here than Katy. If she can't fix her, then she'll tell you so and we can run on into the hospital. Maybe ought to, anyway."

"Ok. Well, I'll try not to worry."

"You mind lending me a hand getting all this loaded up?"

"Not at all. Seems like you have plenty of firewood already, though, don't you?"

"Oh, I do. But it's no good leaving these blow-downs in here; they'll just push other stuff over and pretty soon the deer won't have a way to walk through and they'll quit walking through then the cedars will take over and it won't be worth a dang."

That was a long speech for Art. He stowed the chainsaw in the bed of the truck, right up near the cab, and placed the gas can and hatchet there with it. The two men worked steadily for 15 minutes, loading from smaller to larger. They finally worked together to lever the largest pieces up into the bed, grunting with the effort to balance them on the open tailgate.

"Let's get on back and see how that daughter of yours is getting on," Art said. He started the truck, waited until the power steering pump quit squealing, and drove slowly along the edge of the trees back to the farmhouse.

They left the wood in the truck, brushed the worst of the sawdust from their pants and boots, and went inside the house.

"Katy? Are you two back there?" Art called.

"Yes, we are. You have Mitchell with you?"

"Sure do."

"I think you'll want to see this; come on back," Katy hollered at them.

As they rounded the corner to the bathroom, Carly jumped up and ran straight into Mitchell's arms. Neither man could tell if it was good news or bad news. Mitchell stepped into the tiny room. There was just enough space for him to stand in front of the sink and look down into the tub, where he saw Doug David splashing water on her face, trying to get the paste off her forehead.

"Oh, Mitchell, it worked!" Carly exclaimed. "Katy said we'd have to wait, but Doug David finally just sorta woke up and said her forehead was itchy. She's been trying to wash that off for the last few minutes. She's even hungry, she said!"

"Thank God," Mitchell said quietly. He slumped against the doorframe; his legs suddenly weak. Spots swam in his vision.

"Looks like you wore yourself out there, Mitchell," Art laughed.

"Now, don't make fun of him, Art," Katy said. "He probably hasn't slept a wink since she's been sick." She motioned the men toward the doorway. "Let's leave Carly here to get Doug David dressed, nice and slow, and we all can go see what we can put together for supper."

Art and Mitchell preceded her into the kitchen, and Carly hugged Katy fiercely before allowing her to follow the men, Katy patting her back quietly before she pushed herself away to go cook.

"I was so worried about you, little one," Carly breathed into Doug David's neck as she held her. "I'm glad you feel better."

"I do, but what the heck is that pasty stuff? It feels awful."

"Let's wash you up, ok?"

A mostly-normal bath ensued, and after toweling her off, Carly dressed Doug David in a set of farm clothes Katy had left for her outside the door. The dress was too long for the girl, but it became her favorite that day and she soon grew into it. She wore it at least three times a week from then on.

"All three of our girls wore that dress when they were little. It looks good on you," Katy said with a smile when Doug David and Carly came into the kitchen. "Let's hope you keep wearing it in good health."

Katy had put the men to mashing potatoes and stirring gravy while she built up the fire and warmed the roast from a day ago. She got a loaf of bread out of the box, sliced it, set it on the table with freshly-churned butter. When the five of them gathered, the grace they said was as heartfelt as any they'd said or heard in many years.

Mitchell fell on the food like a starving man would, and Carly had seconds of the mashed potatoes and gravy. Doug David stuck with mashed potatoes and bread with lots of butter. She wasn't back to healthy, but her fever had truly broken.

After they ate, both Mitchell and Carly's eyes fluttered to stay open. Art shared a look with Katy.

"Hey, you two. Why don't you stay here tonight?" Katy asked. "We'll help you watch over the little one and make sure she stays fine. You could use some sleep, I think. Just go on in the back bedroom, slip your shoes off, and get to resting."

Carly and Mitchell didn't argue. Few things are as exhausting as not knowing if a child will live or die and, further, hiding that truth from one's self while trying to minister to the sick. Neither of them had gotten a moment of true rest since Doug David had quit eating two days ago. They collapsed onto the quilted bed, waking in the middle of the night to crawl under the covers and sleep past dawn.

On a spring day soon after the fever, Doug David heard her mama calling her.

"Doug David, I want you to come out here."

"Mama, what?" she replied. "I'm busy getting my doll ready for school."

Carly came around the corner of the porch and stepped inside the screen door to find Doug David, who was sitting on the floor, legs splayed. She had a doll-sized comb in one hand, the doll's hair stretched out in the other. Doug David didn't have any shoes or socks on, and her knees stayed scuffed with farm dirt. She looked up at Carly, grinning.

"Isn't she pretty? Hair is all shiny like mine after you wash it in the rain barrel and comb it for me, huh?"

"She sure is, honey," Carly smiled. "Now leave her to rest a second and come out here; I want to show you something."

Doug David did so, and held Carly's hand while they walked away from the house and into the line of trees that ran along the edge of the property. Five wide-shouldered junipers had formed branches that kept a casual walker out, but Carly pushed through a thick part, holding the branches carefully so they wouldn't slap either of them in the face.

"Mama, I'm getting all buggy and itchy. Why are we going through the trees?"

"You'll see. Just stick with me."

Once past the branches, Doug David found herself inside an open space that felt like a hiding place with only a way out that was straight up. Like if she had a ladder, she could climb out the top and step up onto clouds. She turned a slow circle, peering out to see if she could see the farm, which she couldn't.

"Doug David, this is my secret place. My special place. I come here when I need to think for myself."

"Oh, I love it, mama. Could I share it with you?"

"I hope you will. That's exactly why I brought you out here. You know what a church feels like?"

"Not really."

Doug David knew what a church was. It was a big building that was painted white and had a steep tower in the front. She'd seen the pictures of her mama and dad in front of one, but they hadn't gone to that building since Doug David remembered. So, like a lot of things in her orbit, she knew of a thing but didn't understand it.

"Well, a church is a place where a person can talk to God. Or nature, if you don't tell too many people that it's nature you're talking to and not God," Carly started to explain.

"You're not supposed to talk to God anywhere else? And how do you talk to nature?"

"No, that isn't what I mean, honey. I mean it's a closer place to talk. A place where you can focus. Or at least turn off all the things that are loud so you can hear."

"Like chores?"

"Exactly like chores," Carly said, relieved that she had come up with something that made sense to her daughter.

Part 3

KINGDOM PROPHECY
COMPOUND

CHAPTER TEN

Alaine had left the farm back when he was 19, even though he told the manager of the Feed and Grain Co-op where he asked for a job that he was 21 and could drive a truck wherever the guy needed it. Alaine had to hitchhike over a hundred miles east from the Iowa farm before he got to a place where nobody reacted to it when he said his daddy's name.

He had finally gotten sick and tired of his daddy hitting him. Hitting him for being slow, hitting him for backing the tractor into the stock tank and crimping it, hitting him for sorting the calves wrong. Alaine was big enough to hit back, but there was just something in him that made it impossible to do it. His mother had just stood back and wrung her hands when his daddy got to going; there was no mercy if mother stepped in. Same for his sisters. Daddy would just get tired of whaling on him and he'd take a turn with mother or the sisters if they did anything but keep going with chores.

Stuck with a fury that left him breathless sometimes, Alaine just hugged his mother that day, sketched a wave at his sisters, and started walking down the farm road. Eastbound was his total plan. If his daddy hadn't driven west that morning, he would still be on the farm, cussing at the milk cows to stop bitching and line up. When his daddy hollered, "I'll be back this afternoon" out the truck window, Alaine had reached his limit.

Alaine worked at the co-op for the rest of that season. He stayed on as winter help. He rented a small house out back of a bigger house in the town he'd settled in. The problem was that he didn't trust his boss. He didn't trust his landlord, either. The person he paid rent to, anyway. He wasn't sure if one tiny "barely more than a cabin" in the backyard qualified them as landlords, even though that's what they called themselves. He paid them $150 a month for the house. He didn't have to pay extra for the propane to heat the place or the electricity to cool the place and run the lights, but the landlords bitched at him when he used anything excessive. Which they never defined. But they had tacked on a shower stall to the outside of his small house that included a toilet that flushed. It was usually either too cold or too hot out there, the Great Plains being what they were. He almost preferred the winter because all the spiders died or laid eggs that wouldn't hatch until spring. The landlord told him to "run the heater full blast in the shower house or else them pipes would bust and he'd be shit outta luck."

His boss, Jim, on the other hand, took a real liking to Alaine at the outset. He saw Alaine's bright mind and his ability to work all day and not get lazy. Jim wanted to help him gain enough skill and knowledge so he wouldn't have to work a grain shovel or a silo grain auger all his life. The trouble between them grew from Alaine's interaction with virtually every woman he came in contact with. Which, at a farm co-op in the middle of farm country, isn't that many, but the women who did come in were the kind who took no shit from anyone. They were hardened farm and ranch wives and mothers, and they'd been choosing their battles since they were young girls themselves. So when Alaine, at his age, shot his mouth off about "why aren't you home cooking" or "I noticed your husband could use a new shirt or two" or even "why in the world did a good-lookin' gal like you end up with a pot-bellied sunburned old raisin like him," those women turned right around and went into his boss and gave him hell about the hired help out on the loading dock.

Jim sat him down regularly and talked through each interaction that the women had complained about. He hoped to give Alaine the social skills he sorely needed. All it did was build resentment in Alaine until he was at the familiar point of fury that had caused him to walk off the family farm those several years ago. Alaine had learned a lesson, though, and it was that he wasn't going to be chased off until he had another plan. He played the game, complimented and thanked Jim for helping him see the error of his ways. Alaine promised he'd work harder at getting along with each and every customer. He said he recognized how important community relations were for the success of the co-op, and that those farmers had a choice of where they could take their grain for sale and a choice of where they could buy their next season's seed, their livestock feed, and their animal medicines.

Alaine never did interact very well with the women after Jim's corrective speeches, but he softened his approach enough so they tolerated him. Where Alaine truly shone was with the men who came in. He made a point of memorizing their faces and matching names quickly, he remembered their wives' names, their kids' names, even the names of the dogs that rode along in the truck. Alaine would ask all the right questions about crop health, herd size, pasture leasing. He'd make a point of keeping track of who had land to lease and who needed land to lease, and he'd make the connections for them, even if it took a week or two to finally exchange the information. Alaine started going over to the café to get coffee mid-morning, even though he hated wasting money like that. He would catch the breakfast guys at the tail end, then sit until the lunch guys started to dribble in. Alaine always at the counter, waving cheerily and telling a joke or two. It got so he was kind of a must-see destination in the burg; and, had he been honest with himself, he craved the attention.

Like most fish in very tiny ponds, Alaine eventually outgrew the café, and the co-op, and the old limping ranchers and farmers who had come to rely on his presence in town. As he walked the two blocks home one night, Alaine managed to keep the sneer off his face until he'd passed the kitchen window of his landlord, just in case that old fart windbag was watching as he walked by.

"These people are idiots! I'm not gonna be able to stand it much longer," he swore under his breath.

At the end of the soybean harvest, mid-fall, Alaine told Jim he was moving on. Jim protested and tried to offer first a raise, then a partnership, finally revealing that he was hoping to retire in full in a year or two, and he believed Alaine had what it took to take over. Had Alaine reconsidered right then, he might have turned out OK.

But, as it was, he replied flatly, "Jim, if I have to listen to you screw up one more set of orders over the phone or if I have to be patient and polite to one more dumbass farmer who scuffs in here trying to get a nickel higher per bushel for their crop cuz it's *so superior to the rest*, I'll shoot my foot off and spend the rest of my days in the hospital."

Alaine sneered, "You did what you could for me. You taught me what you knew, which, frankly, was about two days' worth of knowledge that took you all these years to squeeze out of your tiny brain."

"Well, I don't think I appre—"

"I don't give two shits what you appreciate, Jim. You can most assuredly walk down the train tracks and jump in the first stock pond you see, the more turtle shit the better. I'm done taking advice from you and I'm done eatin' the shit these idiots dole out when they come in here. I'm takin' the money from this here till and hittin' the road. Good riddance, you lousy windbag," Alaine spat.

It was Alaine's first experience with how quickly all the good will and good feelings in a curated situation can evaporate. Alaine at least had the awareness to get the hell out of town before Jim recovered enough of his dignity to consider reporting the till money as a crime and sending the sheriff after him.

Alaine saw the city from way far off; he'd heard of skyscrapers and huge buildings and all that, but only from the teacher whose veracity was suspect because, as his daddy had grunted, "she barely goes to church, Alaine, and it's a methodist church, at that." Alaine still had trouble believing people could be good and true and valuable even if they came from, well, something different than daddy trusted.

Alaine had ridden the bus all the way into Chicago. When it parked and the passengers had gotten off and Alaine stood at the corner of a busy street, he almost turned right around and got a ticket back home. Thought maybe he could talk to his daddy and negotiate a truce. Alaine had been gone for almost three years now, and maybe his daddy realized that he needed the help; he wasn't getting any younger. And there was no way his sisters and mother could work all the things that a farm and livestock called for day in and day out. His hunger got the best of him, though, and he walked across the busy street— crosswalks and traffic lights!—to the diner.

Once inside, the waitress nodded her head at an open table and he went to sit in the booth, back to the wall so he could see everyone. The waitress, who introduced herself as Sue, had barely dropped off coffee for him, which he didn't even ask for, when Alaine saw a woman with two little boys come in. Sue tipped her head to them and nodded toward a table in the middle of the diner, catty-corner to Alaine's booth. He didn't let any emotion cross his face, but he mentally rolled his eyes at the grubby faces of the boys and the exhausted, gray face of the woman. He sipped his coffee, ordered a burger and fries, and smiled at the trio when they looked at him after they sat down.

"Now, listen, boys, we're gonna eat something here," the woman said wearily. "But I don't have enough money for you to go crazy, so let me order when she comes over, okay?"

"Mom, we're starving, though!" the older of the two boys whined. "You said we could get whatever we wanted if we were good on the bus and behaved and didn't throw a fit. That's what you said."

The younger boy sat quietly. The corners of his mouth turned down. The tiniest of quivers from his chin.

"Now, Trout, don't do that," the woman said. "There'll be plenty of food! I'm not hungry anyway. Let's look at the menu. Pike, you stop whining and help me pick out something that looks like a lot of food. Can you do that?" she begged.

The boy she called Pike sat up a little straighter and pulled a menu out of the metal rack in the middle of the table. He knocked over the yellow plastic bottle when he did, and it landed on its side, pointing straight at Alaine. A tiny bullet of mustard shot out, traveled across the gap between the tables, and landed on the toe of Alaine's work boot.

"Oh, shit," said the woman. "I'm so sorry! We didn't mean—"

"I'm under attack," Alaine yelled, putting his hands over his head. "I give up!"

Pike laughed at that, and Trout looked over with a grin. The woman smiled then, too, with a grateful face.

"Oh, thank goodness, I don't think I could handle one more person yelling at me about how I need to get my kids under control," she said. "We've been on a bus for days, it seems like, and *some of us* just aren't cut out for the road."

She twitched her fingers at *some of us* and made a tiny nod towards the one she called Pike. Alaine smiled even bigger.

"I'm Alaine. I just got off a bus myself."

"I'm Rosie, and these are my boys Pike and Trout," she replied, placing a hand on each head as she said their names.

Rosie had shoulder-length brown hair with loose curls. She wore a cotton smock with tiny flowers stitched into it, and faded jeans. The rope soles of her espadrilles were frayed and there was a tiny hole in the canvas over each big toe. Pike had a stained striped t-shirt on and jeans; his hair was blonde and rough cut. Trout was dressed in a Celtics basketball tank, jean shorts, and tennis shoes, with his brown hair the same rough cut. His shirt was cleaner than Pike's, but Trout had the remnants of something that looked sticky and sweet all over his chin.

"I'm pleased to meet you three," Alaine smiled, "would you like to join me? I haven't even gotten my food yet. Matter of fact, I kinda want to try at least four of these burgers—how about you boys help me out with that? We can rank them worst to first."

"Listen, Mr. Alaine, you don't need to do that," Rosie resisted. "We're just fine. We don't want to intrude or anything."

"But, mom, he said we could help him! And I'm hungry!" Pike whispered, loud enough for most of the diner to hear.

"Seriously, you'd be doing me a favor," Alaine said, turning on the charm.

He wasn't used to empathy; it had certainly not been a needed emotion for him most of his life. But a chord of it played quietly in him, perhaps an echo of his own mother, downtrodden and exhausted from the cards she'd been dealt, that Alaine had watched her play.

"Please, come sit. It doesn't have to be a big deal," he assured her. "Just some lunch. We've been sitting alone on buses long enough, don't you think?"

Rosie hesitated still, looking first at Alaine, then into each of her boy's faces. Trout looked so hopeful that she couldn't say no to him. Pike tended to complain about almost everything, so he was easier to filter out. But when Trout got that look, like things were finally going his way, she wanted to reward his patient and trusting spirit.

Sue was already moving the rolled silverware to Alaine's table. "What can I getcha, then?" she asked.

After Rosie and the boys shuffled over to the booth to sit down, Rosie across from Alaine and one boy on each side, Alaine said to Sue, "Just pick three of your best burgers with fries to go along with the one I already ordered, would you please?"

Sue looked at the boys, "You two like cheese and pickles and bacon?"

Pike nodded vigorously and Trout said, "Yes, please," in a whisper.

"Hon, would you like a little heat with yours?" she asked Rosie. "We've got a good jalapeño burger if you do?"

"Oh, gosh, no thank you," Rosie replied ruefully. "Those will mess my stomach right up. But a cheeseburger sounds great, please."

"I wouldn't mind the peppers, if you please," Alaine said. "If it's not too much trouble."

"Not at all. Coffee, hon?" Sue said to Rosie. "Milk for the boys?"

"Perfect. Yes, please," Rosie said.

After they'd eaten every scrap of all four plates and had finished off the ice cream that Sue offered to the boys, too, the four of them sat quietly at the table.

"Why don't you two go wash your faces in the bathroom," Rosie said to the boys. "Then use the toilet. Remember to wash your hands again after, please. I'll be right here."

Once they'd left down the short hall to the men's room, Rosie looked at Alaine.

"Now what?"

"I was just about to ask you the same thing!" he laughed. "Where did you say you left from and where did you say you're going?"

Rosie's mouth hardened into a line. "I didn't say either. I don't mean to be rude, but that's going to stay our business for now. Suffice it to say, we're headed west by southwest. Away from here."

"Trouble behind you?" Alaine asked. "Is it still following you?"

She looked worried when he said that. She glanced out the window over at the bus station, turned just as quickly away.

"I'm guessing their dad is missing those boys? Am I right?"

"Dammit," Rosie cursed softly. "It's been days. And we are still obvious. Even to some stranger in a diner. I'm not sure what else I can do except keep going."

Alaine leaned back in the booth. Pushed the toothpick around his teeth.

"I had a thought," he said. "I'm done in. I've got to rest. I didn't have a real plan when I got the bus, but I'm too tired to think past sleep right now."

"And?" Rosie said cautiously.

"My thought was, do you have money for a hotel?"

"I'll thank you to stay out of my finances!"

"Now, look, I don't want anything. But I'm pretty sure that, if you were gonna split one burger between the three of you, that you don't have money to sleep anywhere. I'm just thinking maybe you need some sleep and a good shower and a door that locks."

"Are you asking me to share your motel room?" she marveled.

"Good lord, no! I'm not after that! At all," he insisted. "What I meant was maybe I'd get one room for me. And maybe I could help you out and get one room for you. No strings attached."

"Pardon me, but why the hell would you do that?"

"Mom, don't say that word!" Pike said as he suddenly was back to the table. "You told us it was a bad one."

"Pike, leave mom alone!" Trout ordered. "She's having an adult conversation."

"Well, hello, there, boys," Rosie laughed. "Ah, you do look better. But whew! You could use a fresh set of clothes. Mr. Alaine here just said he would get us a room where we can clean up and rest a little. What do you say?"

Trout looked thoughtfully at her, "Mom, is he still a stranger? Because you said that one thing about strangers."

"I don't guess he's a stranger anymore, Trout," she finally said.

"I should hope not," Alaine added smoothly. "We've had food together! That counts for a lot these days. Plus, it all started cuz I got tired and sleepy while you two were cleaning up."

"We weren't gone that long," Trout objected.

"No, I don't mean that," Alaine agreed. "But I still haven't heard the story of why you two are named after fish, and I simply can't go on with my life without knowing that. And I need the long version, which means I gotta get some rest first."

The boys laughed at that, and Rosie just shook her head, weary again.

Alaine motioned to the waitress. "Let's see if Sue has a place she can send us that won't break the bank." When she came over, he said, "Sue, I'll pay the bill, please. And, if you could be so kind, we'd like directions to a place to stay. Close enough to come back here for breakfast. Is there such a place?"

Sue looked straight at Rosie rather than Alaine, mild alarm on her face. "Is that something you want, ma'am?"

A flash of fury crossed Alaine's face that only Trout saw.

Rosie nodded at Sue and smiled. "It's ok. I don't think he's dangerous. And he said he doesn't want anything for it."

"I'm right here—I can hear you both talking about me," Alaine said. He almost succeeded in keeping the menace from his voice. "I can assure you both that my intentions are honorable. A Good Samaritan, paying back goodwill that I have received."

Had Sue and Rosie come from backgrounds that didn't include troublesome men, they wouldn't have thought another second about it. As it was, Rosie got up, at Sue's urging, and followed Sue behind the counter and into the kitchen.

"Well, boys, I guess they are gonna decide for us, aren't they?" Alaine said. He'd gotten his fury under control and turned it into a bemused curiosity.

In the kitchen, Sue put her hand on Rosie's shoulder. "Listen, tell me now. If you want me to call the cops or if you want to walk out the back or you want me to send Vic out there to send him on his way, I'm good with that."

Rosie leaned against the stainless steel dishwasher, pushed her hands through her hair. "Truth is I don't have much money left. Bus fare to somewhere pretty far short of California, I'd say. And these boys need a break from the bus. He doesn't seem like a bad guy, does he? At least to take one night's motel fare from? I feel like risking it."

"Well. If you think so. Let's do this: if you don't get here by 8 a.m. tomorrow for breakfast, I'll send the cops to the motel. The cops will take our call. The motel will keep an eye out, too. I'll call them after you leave and give them the story. Anything happens... anything at all—you call and we can get you back here. We're always open and I'll leave a note for the night shift."

"That should work. I don't think it'll be a problem, but thank you." Rosie's face had gotten even grayer with fatigue. A tear trickled down each cheek. "I just haven't been able to relax in days! I'm exhausted."

"Come on, then. Let's get you out the door and set up down the block with your 'probably safe knight in shining armor' out there," Sue smiled.

The motel was plain and clean and well-lit and had beds and even a washer and dryer. After the promised breakfast at 8, where Rosie gave the cook a thumbs-up and after a day where they all four did some cautious sightseeing, Alaine ended up convincing Rosie to stay a second night on his tab, separate rooms with no question. After another breakfast, they took the "L", saw the big lake, and the pier. They didn't spend money on the places you had to go into, but it was nice. A respite for Rosie, who had rarely spent a stress-free day with a man. The father of the boys had a temper and a jealous streak that overtook them all almost every day of the seven years she'd been stuck with him.

A rare joy filled Alaine for those two days, enough so he kept the charm going with Rosie, knowing that she would be the decider when he asked them to come with him. For he had decided. The second night in Chicago, loud with trains, cars, bells, sirens, and almost certainly a ripple of gunshots at 3 a.m., convinced him he wasn't a city guy after all. All he had to do was head back west a different direction than the burg he'd left. Alaine would be fine, especially when he got these three to come with him. Not camouflage, exactly, but close. Too close for him to really admit to himself.

The next morning Rosie agreed to travel with him. Alaine promised that he wanted companionship and family. He assured Rosie that she would never need to share his bed; "not that you aren't desirable," he assured her.

"I'm on a quest, I think," he told her. Earnestly. As if he was convincing himself more than her.

"I'll go with you on one condition," she declared with more steel than she ever dared with her ex.

"Name it, Rosie," Alaine said pleasantly.

"You treat these boys as your own. You let them call you daddy if and when they are ready. You don't shame them or beat them." Rosie had started with the steel, but ended almost hissing at him. Realizing it, she stopped and waited to see what his reaction would be.

Alaine was in full damage control mode, though, and figured she'd say something along those lines, so he was able to keep his face composed throughout.

"I'll do ya one better, Rosie. I'll do all that—no problem—and I won't shame or beat you, either. Do we have a deal?"

He stuck his hand out, smiled at her, and they shook on it.

It would take them five years to work their way onto the Fox Farm, and by that time the boys did indeed call Alaine daddy. Alaine had never once asked Rosie to lay with him. He had begun to read the Bible during year two, and had stuck almost exclusively to the Old Testament by year three. They averaged about a year per rental place before the landlord and Alaine scrapped over one thing or another. Alaine convinced Rosie each time that they were the wronged party and that it wasn't fair and that, rather than stay and fight where they weren't wanted, they should move on and start fresh.

On the eve of the last move Alaine would ever make, Rosie pulled the boys aside. "Listen, you two. You're old enough now. Do we give it one more try with him? Or do you want to strike out on our own?"

Pike immediately said, "I want to go with Alaine. We just need to find people who understand what we are after!"

Trout took longer to answer. "I'm okay to go along, mom. He's not perfect, but he has cared for us this long. Maybe it's better than trying to figure it all out on our own?"

Rosie shook her head and said, "Yeah, you're probably right. It's a mess either way, but maybe less trouble if we stick with him and hope the next place is where we can truly settle."

CHAPTER ELEVEN

About the time Carly showed Doug David the secret place, Alaine stomped across the property; not angry, but in the way of conquest and discovery. When he and his band of three had decided once again to move, this farm, with possibilities for a small ranch, seemed the perfect size. It was situated along the Ninnescah River, that flowed west to east, carried some volume, but was a backwater. On this humdrum river, Alaine felt it would be easy to build a life out of time along its banks. Oh, not *easy;* it would be years of backbreaking work. But *easy* as in purity of purpose, clarity of task, unity of his band. Mostly, it was out of the way, and he hoped he could, finally, be in charge with no one to wreck it.

Alaine crested a rise in the long bluegrass that ran right up to the start of the juniper trees that lined the river. Birds ate the juniper berries and then shat the seeds as they rested on the barbed wire fence after a good meal. Those seeds grew into the windbreak he was looking at. He also saw the ranks of young trees edging the property, deliberately planted, that would serve better than man-made fencing.

"Perfect to keep prying, unclean, mistrustful eyes from watching our evolution," Alaine said aloud to himself.

He spread his legs wide, and planted his fists on his waist, turned his bearded face to the sun. Glared at it, then softened his face with a smile.

"Yes. This will do. This is where I will make my stand. I will praise your Name with a cairn of stones, just like Your people did in the Old Testament. Here I raise my Ebenezer."

The reality that another couple lived there already didn't bother him; the anticipation of winning them over by the end of the day, and his convincing them to extend an invitation to live with them on the property, widened his smile. He flexed his stomach muscles, clenched his fists, shook them at the sky in triumph. Everything he saw was his.

"Mitchell, there's a man on the porch," Carly said calmly. "And it's not Mr. Gfeller, either."

"Well, does he look dangerous? Angry? Like an official?" Mitchell was slurping tomato soup from a pot, ravenous from a morning of work on the property. Doug David had already eaten her plain cheese sandwich, dipped in soup, and had gone back to her room to put her flowers in the sun. The puppy, Skip, dozed on its old blanket in the corner of the kitchen, tucked back between the cupboards and the stove.

"I have no idea, Mitchell. But would you please go deal with him? I don't want to."

Mitchell, wiping his beard to make sure tomato soup hadn't camped there, threw his cloth napkin down on the table. He hit the edge of the table with his leg as he stood and strode to the front door. It wasn't locked; of course it needn't be, this far removed from others. It was closed, though, because the screen door had a few holes that Mitchell hadn't gotten around to patching yet, and the flies somehow knew they could torment live humans as soon as they found their way into the house.

Mitchell wasn't at all pleased to see anyone. He'd made his peace with Gfeller, but no one else. Mitchell had gotten worse as a leader, if that was possible; he'd tamped down his inadequacies about how to run his life, a farm, a family. He knew that taking it out on Carly wasn't an option; she watched him too closely ever since DD was born. The pressure on him to perform, to excel, had turned into steam under pressure, looking for a weak spot in him to split his skin and erupt. This unwanted visitor caused a seam of pressurized angst to grow just under his calm; Mitchell found himself spoiling for a fight, just as release.

The man on the porch had a nice enough smile, though, and his arms were spread wide to show he meant no harm.

"I promise, I'm not selling anything," Mitchell heard the man say.

Doug David had come out of her room and stood in the hallway with a view of the door, but protected from being seen from the porch. She had a feeling in the pit of her stomach like she did right before a thunderstorm throws everything at them.

"I've got a good feeling about your farm, sir," the man said. "And I'd like to talk to you about buying it."

"Farm's not ours to sell. We're caretakers, really," Mitchell said, swinging the door closed.

The man reached out, stopped the travel of the door, smiled even wider.

"I've got money. I've got connections. Perhaps I could take just a minute of your day and introduce myself?"

"I'll come out." Over his shoulder, Mitchell called back toward the kitchen, "Carly, I'll be out on the porch. Keep the door shut."

He didn't wait for a response from Carly, and he stepped through the doorway, motioning to his right for the man to sit. Mitchell perched on the railing, wanting to send a message to the man that he wasn't getting comfortable.

Watching from a window, Carly and DD could see Mitchell's face but not the other man's. Mitchell had a dark expression. His lips were pressed tightly together. He held his hands folded, but the skin looked white from his grip.

Doug David had tiptoed down the hallway and into the front room. She could not hear what they were saying to each other, but the visitor did most of the talking. He used his hands a lot, and he laughed now and then. It was a merry sound, and she felt happier when she heard it. Like birds singing, or water burbling past reeds. Maybe she'd show the man those reeds at the river.

"Mama, who is that man?"

"Doug David, I don't know. Let's just stay in here and hope he goes away."

"Okay, mama."

In the back of Carly's mind was that niggling wish for someone to take over being in charge. So Mitchell wouldn't get how he gets with the stress and forehead and the sunken eyes. She never expected it to happen, though, and now that this guy was clearly giving his pitch to Mitchell, she doubted.

Carly and DD sat for a time, watching the men talk. Mitchell had moved from the porch rail to the porch chair close to the man. Mitchell's face had since cleared, and he was talking now, too. He used his hands and swung them wide then bringing them into a circle. He smiled at the man. Carly and DD could hear Mitchell's tone of voice turn to encouraging, but they couldn't make out the words.

As Mitchell's face grew lighter, Carly's grew darker. As Mitchell's mouth relaxed, Carly's tightened until her lips were pressed tightly into a single, bloodless line. Carly pulled DD into her body, draped her arms around DD's shoulders. A fly buzzed around Doug David's head; she waved her hand, lazily, at it. Just like her father did when a fly got in.

The two men stood, shook hands, and came inside.

Mitchell said with an excited look on his face, "Carly, I'd like you to meet Alaine. He's going to rent space out back."

"Is that so?" Carly replied.

"It is. He has a lot of ideas that I think can help us."

Mitchell breathed heavily, like he'd just run a race. He smiled at Carly, then looked down and smiled at Doug David. He kept raising his arms up near his shoulders, as if he were either lifting something to heaven or celebrating a win. Carly couldn't tell which.

The man named Alaine stepped forward, his arm outstretched to shake her hand. He had a wide smile on his face and his eyes, a startling blue, were the clearest she'd ever seen. She put her hand out, reflexively, and allowed him to take her hand in both of his. She wondered if he was a warlock, because she already felt like she was under a spell and powerless to resist him. An image flashed through her mind of a wizard from the Renaissance fairs she used to frequent.

"Hello, ma'am. My name is Alaine. I know your husband—a fine man—told you that, but I believe in good manners. I've got nothing but admiration for your property, and this man of yours has a good head on his shoulders. Me and my few people can't wait to share the labor to bring this land to its full fruition and glory," he finished with a flourish. He tried to lift Carly's hand to his lips, but she drew it back quickly. Held it clenched with the other to her chest.

"You have people?" Mitchell asked, sounding surprised. "It's a small property."

"Oh, did I not mention that?" Alaine said as if it were the slightest oversight. "Yes, I have a wife—well, a common law wife; I don't believe the state needs to know we are a family—and two young boys," he added with a relaxed air.

"We surely don't have room for you all to stay in the house," Carly objected. "And, Mitchell, maybe we could—"

Mitchell held his hand up to her face, stopping her, while using his other hand to make an onward motion to Alaine.

"Of course not," Alaine assured her. "We have tents—big Army surplus canvas ones. Just as good as a cabin! And I'll vow to you this very day that we will have our own home built within a week. Providing you can help Mitchell out with things around here so he can assist us now and then? The wall-raising is a mite scary with just a woman and two boys."

"Uh, I—" Carly started, but then stopped speaking, her mouth hanging open. She looked at Mitchell, who looked back at her with an encouraging face, smiling widely. Willing her to agree to the terms that, apparently, both Mitchell and Alaine wanted.

"Mitchell?" Carly asked, hoping he would see her discomfort, but not wanting to make either of these men angry.

"We've got a good handle on the fall chores, so I'll have plenty of time to help you, sir," Mitchell said. He ignored Carly's question.

"Good, then that's settled!" Alaine exclaimed. "And who is this young lady?"

Carly kept her arms over the shoulder of Doug David, who scooted back into the folds of Carly's skirt, a wary look on her face.

"This is our daughter."

Alaine lowered himself into a squat, down to her level, put his hand out to her. A full-wattage smile. He managed to hide all of his guile and his conquest and his plans from his face. A chameleon wanting to hide.

"I'm Alaine. I bet you'll love having my two boys to play with. Won't you?"

Doug David's eyes got wide, and she chewed on her forefinger. She didn't say anything. She didn't risk a glance up at her mother to see what she thought about playmates. She thought of four places that she would love to show someone else, and the idea of showing his two boys filled her with pride on the one hand, and a vague unease on the other. Finally, she put her hand out and shook Alaine's.

As soon as she saw Alaine and Mitchell cross the yard towards the river, DD rushed out the front door. She ran to the glade, Skip trailing after her, nose to the ground. DD pushed through the trees impatiently. Plumped to the ground on the long grass in the middle. Skip nudged her a few times then laid down along her leg, panting from the trot.

DD was upset but didn't know why. Something about that man made her nervous. Like when it was about to thunder and lightning. Or like on cold days when the sun quit shining and snowflakes started batting at the front window.

Pretty soon, DD heard her mama through the branches.

"DD? You out here?"

She didn't answer; just sat still with Skip at her side. Skip looked up and back over his shoulder at Carly's arrival but didn't move either.

"Why'd you run off, little one?" Carly asked when she entered the clearing.

DD sniffled. "That guy. I don't like him."

Carly said nothing of her own grave misgivings about the man; she wanted to present a united front with Mitchell. And she didn't want DD to have to worry about anything while she was just a little girl.

"Really? I don't think he's gonna be much of a bother. I wish we could have talked it through first without him standing there like he owned the place, but daddy's smart. He won't let anything bad happen."

"That's what *you* think."

"Yes, that's what I think. Don't be mean; it doesn't suit you, DD," Carly admonished. "I'll talk to daddy, though. Make sure knows how we both feel. OK?"

"I guess," DD said peevishly.

CHAPTER TWELVE

Carly had known, from the day that Alaine stepped onto the porch, that something was off about the arrangement Mitchell had made with him to live on their property. She also knew right away that, out of the four adults—herself, Mitchell, Alaine, Rosie— the vote was going to be three to one on anything significant. Mitchell telling her that she would have the run of the house and could make all the "important domestic decisions" didn't fool her for one second. Carly met Alaine's partner, Rosie, the morning after Alaine had talked himself onto the property.

"Hello, my name is Carly," she began, after walking out to the canvas tent and approaching the woman cooking over a fire.

"Rosie," she said in a clipped tone. Rosie had stood up with the wooden stirring spoon still in her hand, runny eggs dripping from the end. She had on a skirt and a t-shirt, neither of which looked particularly clean or new.

"Can I do anything to help you settle in?" Carly looked around at the campsite, which was already littered with clothes on bushes and food boxes and cans in messy stacks near the fire.

"Alaine made it very clear to us that we aren't to come bother you at the house," Rosie said grimly.

She was angry. Carly could tell by the way she sat abruptly back down to dash the spoon into the scrambled eggs. By the way she flipped the bacon in the other skillet.

"I'd have thought he'd at least gotten us permission to wash!" Rosie finished.

"Who in the world told you that you couldn't wash?" Carly asked in disbelief.

Rosie looked straight up at Carly, pointed the spoon. "You did."

Carly took a step back and raised her hands in defense. "I said no such thing!"

"Even if that were true, and Alaine made his own rules—which wouldn't be the first time—you didn't exactly lay out the welcome mat for us here, now did you?" Rosie complained.

Carly was taken aback. She thought back to the front porch, the day before, and the conversation she'd been a part of—barely—where Alaine said he had others and Carly had objected to them staying in the house.

"Well, try and see it from my point of view," Carly began. "We've lived out here for years and haven't had hardly any guests—"

"Your choice, is what I hear," Rosie said under her breath.

"—and now this messy bearded man traipses up and just tells us he's gonna move in. That's not normal. Not by a long shot," Carly said with some heat. "And if you just dawdle along behind him wherever he goes, knowing good and well that he's got nothing of his own—does he—and just plunk down where he says to, isn't normal, either."

Rosie glared at Carly. Looked like she was going to spit on her. Rosie said with menace, "You've made your position very clear, I'd guess. And don't worry, I won't be asking for any of your precious farmhouse resources! Alaine's made some iffy choices over our time together, but he's the wagon I'm hitched to and if you think that's not normal, then too bad for you. I'd invite you to stay for breakfast, but I just don't want to spend any more time with you."

At that, Rosie turned away from Carly and hollered, "Boys! Come eat while it's hot! We've got a lot to do today."

Carly stood in shock, her mouth wide open and hands at her waist. "Rosie, All I came over to say is—"

"Oh, you've been quite clear. Do us a favor and go back to your palace," Rosie sneered.

Carly stood for a moment more. But Rosie had perfected her silent treatment and refused to even acknowledge that she was still there. One of the tent flaps flipped open and a boy emerged. Another boy rounded the corner of the second tent, buttoning his trousers as he came to the fire.

"Smells great, mom!" said one.

"I'm starved," said the other.

They both looked at Carly, then at Rosie, then at each other. They shrugged and took the plates full of breakfast from Rosie. They sat on the camp stools and ate quietly. Carly turned on her heel and left, her cheeks red in anger and embarrassment.

Carly ended up walking over to the glade, which had already become her strategy space to deal with the invading horde. She took both solace and silence when she came in there, listening for the Word of God that would guide her out of this weird new life and protect her only living child. There was no chance she would hear from God today. Not after that encounter. She'd intended to find common ground with Rosie and maybe even make a friendly alliance.

"You'd think two mothers could find something in common, wouldn't you?" she said out loud. "Can't be the first time mothers needed to team up!"

She heard a rustling from one of the cedars across the glade, looked over, saw Skip bounding toward her and DD ducking out of her hiding spot within a hiding spot to come over.

"Oh, hi, mama. We've been hiding and thinking," DD smiled.

"Yeah? What are you hiding from? Wait—what are you thinking about?" Carly decided to ask first.

"I've been thinking if I want to share with those boys. Did you meet them yet?" DD asked with a frown.

Carly pursed her lips and shook her head. "I saw them. Just now. But I didn't stay to meet them, because they were eating breakfast. I met their mom," she added sourly.

"What's her name?" DD asked.

"Her name is Rosie. And I don't think she likes us. Wait, that's not fair. She's new here and scared and didn't say very nice things to me when we met. I'm going to try again later to make friends with her," Carly said in an effort to be judicious.

"She better be nice to you! She's a visitor, and she's supposed to have manners," DD recited, as if her mother had asked her for the right response.

Carly sat on the soft grass in the glade, patted the ground beside her. Skip flopped down where Carly had patted, and DD sat right next to him, laughing at her pup. Carly looked over at DD, softened her expression from the morning of angst. "Remember when I said I want you to share this place with me, Doug David?"

"I do, mama. Is this a place we can be honest? Or a place where you are always right?"

Carly started to speak, her mouth already open, then stopped. "DD, I'm not always right. Why do you say that?"

"You tell me that. Sometimes. When I argue," DD finished quietly.

It was a big concept for a young girl to navigate, and Carly knew this mundane conversation, like so many small moments, would affect the rest of their lives together. She focused her thoughts before she spoke.

"DD, what if—what if this? When we are here, in our glade, we can be truthful and honest with each other. As long as our words are loving?"

DD looked up at her mama, hopeful, looking to see if she really meant it or it was more of a parental "someday" kind of talk. Carly held DD's gaze, clear-eyed, a look of love washing her face.

"I like that idea, mama. Let's try it."

Thus it was decided that they would have a safe place, a place of mediation and arbitration, though neither thought of those words.

"I guess that means we can say honest things about the new visitors, but we have to try and be polite about them," Carly summarized. "It seems like a bad idea to me now, for them to live here, but maybe we can get to know them and it will be better."

DD looked at her doubtfully, but said, "If you say so. We should try and make friends, at least. Right?"

"You got it, little one." Carly hoped she'd hidden her dislike well enough that DD didn't pick up on it.

Doug David slowly laid back down in the glade, her legs crossed and her hands in her lap. She looked around at the green walls accented with frosty-blue juniper berries. She lifted one leg at a time and set her heels back down, moving them a little to make divots to rest in. After a minute, she reached a hand up and pointed.

"A cloud, mama. And a hawk circling under it. I wouldn't have seen that if I was just running around or playing with my doll. I like this place."

CHAPTER THIRTEEN

Four days after Alaine met them all, the skeleton of a simple building had indeed risen in the back quarter of the property. He'd driven two borrowed trucks down the road and into the long grass past the farmyard, both of them full of building materials. The cottonwood held down one corner of the property, and the new building made the third angle of a triangle with the farmhouse that Doug David, Mitchell, and Carly lived in.

A worn footpath soon ran between the new building and the farmhouse. Doug David had graduated from watching them work through the window, to sitting on the back porch, and, today, to walking over there to see what was going on up close. The two boys had hammers and were tacking pieces of board to the lower vertical parts of the building that Alaine had put up. The boys stopped when she walked up to them.

"What are you doing here?" one of them asked.

"I came to see what you are doing," Doug David told him.

"Papa said you have a boy's name," said the other.

"No I don't. It's just my name."

Well, my name's Pike, and my brother's name is Trout. Those are boy names. Our mom is Rosie. That's a girl name."

"Those are fish names, not boy names."

"You shut up," Pike snapped. "Daddy says those are boy names, and that fish are named after us." His blonde hair had streaks of mud in it. He wore overalls with no shirt underneath. He was barefoot.

"You shouldn't say shut up. That's a mean thing," Doug David recited.

"We're allowed to say that if we hear something stupid, Daddy says," countered Trout, whose brown hair looked cleaner than Pike's. He wore shorts that still had the word "flour" on them, running sideways down his leg. He had a t-shirt on that was too big for him, and there were two big rips in it across his back.

"Stupid isn't a nice word, either," she said.

The three children had reached an impasse. The two boys weren't sure if they should turn back to their work, and leave their backs unprotected against this girl, or keep facing her, leaving them unprotected against their Daddy's wrath if he saw them not working. A steady hammering and grunting came from the far side of the building.

"Daddy said we need to keep working, so if you want to help you can bring us boards from that stack over there," Trout said with little expectation of assistance. "But he told us it was our responsibility to get done today."

"I guess I could help," she said doubtfully.

"Well, get to it then," Pike ordered.

Doug David glared at the boy because he didn't have any manners, but he had already turned back to his work, putting three nails in his mouth and closing his lips over them. She didn't think that looked very clean. She turned and went to the pile of flat boards, picking two that were short and light and carrying them across her forearms back to the boys. She waited, not sure what to do.

Pike hammered a third nail into a board, turned to her, looked at the boards she held, sneered.

"Well, put 'em down, then. It'll take us all day if you only carry two at a time," Pike griped at her.

"Geez, Pike," Trout said. "Take it easy. That's two less than we have to carry," he added, just loud enough for Doug David to hear.

She dropped the boards, returned to the pile, carried more, dropped them. She did this for at least 45 minutes and got several splinters in the process that sent lances of fire up her arms. Sweat had stained her favorite dress, and dirty wood chips had gotten in the folds of it, too.

"I'm quitting. See ya," she announced.

Her arms had begun to sting enough that she was worried she would start crying. She didn't want these boys to see her cry.

"Pretty early to be quittin', don't ya think?" Pike groused. "There's a whole pile left to move."

"She can quit when she wants to, Pike. Leave her alone," Trout said back. "Thanks for the help, um, Dougie Dave."

"It's not Dougie Dave. It's Doug David," she said over her shoulder on the way to the house. Her voice stayed steady, but the tears had begun to fall as she walked away.

When Doug David got back to the house from helping the boys, she found her mother in the kitchen.

"Mama, why do I have boy's names?"

Carly put down the knife she was using to peel carrots and potatoes, and dried her hands on her apron. She stepped to the fridge, pulled out the lemonade, and poured a glass. She set it on the table, along with a plate of crackers and grapes.

"Come sit, little one. Have a drink and a snack. You look like you've been working hard."

"Yeah, I helped those boys. They told me I have a boy name. But they have fish names."

"Oh, that's right. Trout? and what's the other?"

"Pike. Trout and Pike. Seems dumb."

"Well, sweetheart, parents name their children all kinds of things for all kinds of reasons. Why, I knew a boy who had the name Sue, and he took no end of—"

"But, mom, why do I have boy names?"

Carly heaved a deep sigh, rubbed her forehead, smoothed her hair back. Sat lost in thought.

Doug David had eaten two crackers and three grapes during the time her mother sat there, but she knew her mama did that sometimes, and it was easiest to let her come back on her own. Doug David swung her legs back and forth under the table, feeling a little better with some food in her stomach.

"You, my sweet thing, are named after your older brothers," Carly finally said.

"I have brothers? Where are they?" DD exclaimed. "Why aren't they here?"

"You do have brothers, except they live in—well, they died."

Carly's voice had taken on a gentle, purring tone, one that Doug David rarely heard. It made the words her mama was saying less scary, and less confusing, and allowed her a chance to ask another question. Sometimes her mama's voice, and a lot of times her dad's voice, was tough and crackly and then she knew she wasn't supposed to ask anything else.

"Did they die before I was born? Is that why I don't know them?" DD saw the sadness in her mama's face.

"Yes, that's exactly right, love. When we first moved out here, I had them in my belly. I must've worked too hard, or God must've needed—well, I had them and they didn't live, is all," Carly managed to say.

Carly was looking out the window, her fingertips moving back and forth along the tabletop. She felt the tears start, and she noticed when DD saw her start to cry.

"Where did you put them then?" DD asked, starting to cry because her mother was crying.

"You remember my favorite place out by the river? Under the cottonwood?" Carly pointed out the window and held the pose, a beseeching look on her face.

"Sure, I do. It's my favorite place, too."

Carly smiled and laughed a short laugh through tears, "Of course it is, right? That is my favorite place because that is where your father and I buried both of those boys."

"You mean you put them in the ground?" Doug David said with alarm.

Carly was nodding before DD even finished her short question. She pantomimed swaddling and hugging and laying the tiny ones down on the ground, using the table as the burial site.

"I do. That's what you are supposed to do when someone dies."

DD had sat straight up while Carly went through the motions, her eyes widening at each step. She used her hands to pat the air right next to her.

"So all this time when I sit there they are underneath me?"

Carly smiled a brittle smile with more tears. She shook her head this time, trying to diminish DD's fears.

"Honey, they are not underneath you. Only their bodies are. The things that made them your brothers are in another place, a better place," she tried to explain. "Your father and I wanted a place to remember them at, and we didn't want to have to leave the farm to go sit with them—with their memory, I mean."

Carly wasn't sure if that made any sense to DD, and felt frustrated.

DD seemed frustrated, too. She had folded her arms and frowned when she said, "Well, where's that? Can we go there? I want to see them."

Carly stopped herself from losing her temper. She took a deep breath. "No. It's not a place we can go. I really wish we could, though, that's a great idea, sweetheart."

DD still looked doubtful. She, too, took a deep breath and looked her mama square in the eye, "I'm not sure that is going to be my favorite place anymore. I'll have to see how I feel next time I go out there," she declared.

Carly felt relieved and said, "And that's OK. I was waiting until you asked about it to tell you." Carly wondered, for the millionth time, if waiting for DD to ask was the right move, or if she and Mitchell should have told her about the boys from DD's earliest days. For now, it seemed enough.

Doug David sat for a minute, finished her crackers, then her grapes, then her lemonade before saying, "I've got splinters in my arms. They hurt."

"Goodness, let me see!" Carly took DD's arms in her hands and turned them palm up. "Oh, gosh, I bet those do hurt. One second; I'll get something to help."

Carly went to the hall closet where she pulled the first aid kit out, plus a washcloth. She came back into the kitchen, wet the cloth, sudsed it up with soap, and wrung it out.

DD had returned her arms to her lap below the tabletop.

"OK, show me your arms again," Carly said. "Nurse Mama is here to fix you right up."

DD chuckled at that. She stuck her arms straight out from her chest, palms up, lifting them above the table. A few red welts showed along her forearms, and Carly saw three or four splinters she could pull out.

"These are tweezers," she said, holding them up. "I can use them to pull the pieces of wood out, remember? Just rest your arms on the table. That'll be easier."

"Yeah, I remember." A quaver shaded her voice.

"If you can be brave, I'll tell you why we gave you your name. Deal?"

Doug David nodded, looking at her mother, and not down at her arms. Carly worked quickly, pulling the tiny splinters out first, swabbing both arms with the washcloth, painting a thin layer of mercurochrome along each spot, and finishing with a band-aid. She lifted her daughter to her lap, hugging her tightly and burying her nose in her hair.

"That wasn't so bad, was it?" Carly reassured her.

"No, I guess not! I'm just glad it's over. I'm not helping those dumb boys anymore," she sniffled.

Carly laughed. She stroked DD's hair and pulled her back into her chest. They both still sat the table where they could look out the window at the clouds scudding by. Carly spoke softly in almost a whisper, "You are named Doug for your first brother, and named David for your second brother. They were twins, so they were born at the same time. I was terribly sad at the time, so I prayed that, if I could have another baby, I promised to name them after the twins. So I could remember them."

"So I *do* have a boy's name," DD said in triumph. But a respectful win; she didn't want to start a fight about her attitude.

Carly admitted with a smile, "Well. I guess you do. But... *your* name is precious because it has three people in it, and not just one like everyone else. You know how much we love you, right?"

Carly squeezed her even tighter in a hug. DD hugged her mama's arms around her.

"You love me a *lot.*"

"That's right, we do," Carly said, weeping again. "We love you more than anything else, and since you have your brother's names, we can love all three of you like that."

That DD carried three people's love inside her didn't scare her; it felt like a privilege. A special thing. Exactly what Carly had hoped when she breathed the prayer to God for another child.

"Ok. I guess I understand. At least it's better than being named for a fish," DD laughed.

"Maybe you should ask them why they got their names from fish. I bet there's a good story there," Carly chuckled.

She stood up and lifted DD to her feet. They both unwittingly mimicked each other by shaking their hair out and smoothing their skirts.

DD twitched one side of her mouth up and said, "Maybe. I was going to show them my favorite spot by the river under the tree, but now I'm not sure. Maybe I won't. The one named Pike is pretty mean," she admitted.

"Well, you do what you think is right. And only if you're comfortable with it," Carly told her.

Carly glanced out the window, saw where the sun was, and jumped back to her feet. "Want to help me get going on dinner?" she asked DD. "Your daddy will be back soon. And, I was thinking, maybe we could make enough to take out to our visitors."

CHAPTER FOURTEEN

Rosie hadn't meant to be so brusque with the woman when she came over to their camp. But it was always rough when Alaine began a new mission. She'd taken to using his terminology about their moves, which was easier than facing the truth about the dysfunction. Rosie thought back to when she and her little boys left Brooklyn. It had been over five years ago, and she felt like she was still on the run from her ex, Doyle. He'd done most of his husbanding and parenting with his fists. Rosie still felt like it was the right move to leave Doyle, to leave Brooklyn, to leave the city where she'd felt at home. At the moment, though, with that hag of a woman Carly trying to ingratiate herself, Rosie wished for the anonymity of the busy city streets. In New York, she minded her own business and all the other millions of people minded their own.

Rosie lived with Doyle in the basement of a small house. They rented from the lady upstairs, who had some weird former relationship with Doyle, but he was so earnest in his commitment to her that Rosie had no choice but to take him at his word and move in. She had already left her fifth floor walkup after her roommate told her to get out because her boyfriend was moving in. The roommate couldn't resist telling Rosie that she was sick of her anyway, and glad for the excuse to ask her to leave. Rosie had no choice there, either; she gathered a suitcase and two boxes of stuff, flipped her roommate off, and walked to the diner where she worked. The cook let her store her pathetic life in the office, but gave her only a day to get it gone to somewhere else.

Rosie was embarrassed that three containers were all she had to her life. She sat and had a cup of coffee. After that was gone, she still had three hours before her shift started, so she went walking. It was on the walk that she ran into Doyle. He didn't lead with his selfish, narcissistic traits; she'd have steered clear if he had.

"What's your game plan here, mister," she said to him after two weeks of attention.

"I've got a plan, for sure, Rosie," he chuckled. "It mostly involves me convincing you that I'm the guy for you, and you're the gal for me."

She'd been in a ratty motel for two weeks, basically trading her paycheck for the weekly charge. She ate leftovers from the diner and usually got a free meal from the cook, who saw that she was down on her luck. Rosie spent her nights crying herself to sleep at the motel, wishing she could figure out a better way, a better thing to do, that would take her out of this dead-end spiral.

"Is this what other people have to go through before their luck turns better?" she'd ask the walls.

Doyle promised her a house with a yard and pets and kids and groceries and maybe even two cars and evenings with them home and enjoying each other's company in a peaceful life. It depressed her even more when she realized that her acceptance to Doyle's ploy was a cliché; she swallowed the bait of his offer hook, line, and sinker. He was a model husband all the way through the birth of Pike and well into the infant-hood of Trout, both named at Doyle's insistence—more of the inane fishing cliché. He told Rosie that his grandfather yarned all the time about how great the fishing was upstate, and that someday he would take them all there. Rosie, by now, knew there was little chance of that, but allowed him to claim the naming rights because she thought it was smart to let him have his way without argument. Normal names, though? More than once she wished she'd insisted on them.

Doyle's bursts of anger started over some kind of trouble at his job with the Transit Authority. He never explained to her what had happened. She only knew that he had to work second shift, which meant he slept until noon, left the house at two, and didn't get home until usually two the next morning. Any fool knows that a Transit shift isn't 12 hours, even with a commute into and out of the city, but she got nowhere when she asked.

"Where I am is none a your damned business, woman," he ranted. "I work my ass off for you and these spoiled kids, and I'll get home when I get home!"

"We miss you, is all," Rosie whined. "It's so fun when you are here—the boys just watch that door waiting for you to get back."

She tried to inject some actual joy into those words, but she didn't fool Doyle and she didn't fool herself, either. Another few months passed of Doyle playing his overworked and absentee father act. When he did begin to leave later and come back sooner, he got physical with her. It started by him shoving past her in the kitchen. It escalated to grabbing her arm and pulling her or pushing her out of the way.

"Why are you always in my way, Rosie?" he'd yell.

"I'm making you lunch, like you asked," she'd yell back.

She'd flinch then, because his usual answer was non-verbal. He didn't care if she bruised; he didn't care when she asked him to stop; he didn't care when she threatened to call the police.

When the kids were seven and five, she'd had enough. Rosie made plans to leave. It would take money, which she had none of, and it would take stealth, which she thought she could manage. In all the years they lived in that basement, she hadn't done much more than say hello to the landlady upstairs. Rosie decided she would change that; she went up to the front porch and knocked on the door.

"I wondered," said the landlady without further address.

"Wondered what?"

"How long you'd last with that lump of a man. Please tell me you're leaving."

Rosie suddenly felt flustered. "I'm sorry. You've got me at a loss. I'm Rosie, and I'm sure sorry I've never come said hello before now."

Rosie stuck her hand out to shake.

"My name's Betty. Doyle's first wife," the landlord said equably. "I'll give you a second; it's weird."

Betty came out onto the porch and sat on the metal glider rocker. There wasn't room for Rosie on it, though there might have been if Betty had scooched to one side. Rosie stood on the porch with a puzzled look on her face.

"It was simpler to keep the house in the divorce and just ignore each other. I wasn't gonna sell my half to him and he's no smarter than a brick. I told him to shut up and take the basement and we didn't have to mess with alimony or splitting the mortgage or anything. I worked it so he rents from me, and I keep the house," Betty said with satisfaction.

"Wow. I didn't know any of that. Not one bit of it."

Betty laughed. She made a shooing motion with her hands and said, "Don't take it too hard. You've lasted long enough. I don't blame you for wanting to get gone."

"How'd you know that I want to leave?" Rosie felt both curious and ashamed.

"Oh, you've got the look," Betty assured her. "And, no, I won't tell Doyle. He likely won't notice right away. After a day or two, sure. But you'll get a head start."

Rosie added a look of relief to her confusion. "Well, I'm glad to hear that. But I still don't fathom how you picked up on those clues."

"You're not a silent movie down there," Betty admitted. "I heard all his changes as they came. Pretty similar to how it went for us. I guess I maybe oughta come down and talked it over with you while he was gone," she said with some shame. "Girls stick together. I didn't do a good job with that."

Rosie widened her eyes in surprise. "You didn't owe me anything! I had no idea who you were. I think it's my fault. For not coming to say hello, at least. Not bringing the boys up with a May basket or cookies or something. I'm pretty hopeless at girl friendships."

Betty slapped her hands together, like she was ready to start a chore. "Welp, let's figure out a way to get you on your way, then, shall we?"

Rosie took two weeks to slowly gather clothes and papers into a cloth bag that she kept in the closet. Not enough to draw Doyle's attention. Still, it wouldn't have worked at all if Betty hadn't given her $300 and said, "Take the bus. Just go west. Chicago ought to be a good enough start."

"You mean it? I can't pay you back; you know that, right?"

Betty's face softened and she laid her hand on Rosie's arm. "Just do the right thing for someone else someday; that's all you can do. We'll call this a returned security deposit." Betty smiled at Rosie and pulled her into an awkward hug.

Rosie sniffed away a tear or two and said, "You may have saved our lives, Betty. Thank you."

Right after Doyle left for his next shift, Rosie and the boys walked up the basement steps, out the side door, and towards the closest bus stop. They rode the bus to the train station and from there left Brooklyn forever.

Rosie recounted the whole story in her mind as she sat there after the breakfast blowout with Carly. She was ashamed of herself at remembering what Betty asked her to do—the right thing for someone else. After she'd cleaned up the camp breakfast, she went in search of Carly, determined to set things right.

They didn't actually meet up until dinner time. Alaine had needed Rosie to do a bunch of mindless chores that he called "important to our success."

"As if laundry and cleaning the truck out and making the beds, which are sleeping bags, anyway, matters to our success," she groused. She did the work, though. She owed him that much. No matter how much she realized that he wasn't perfect and was very possibly a huge problem she'd have to deal with someday, he still was her rescuer. One phone call, she thought, is all it would take from Alaine for Doyle to find out where she and the boys were.

"I can't risk it; I just can't," she'd say to herself in a listless, defeated voice. More than once a day, though she never realized how often she gave up.

As Rosie walked back from the river where she'd had a sponge bath after finishing the chores, she saw Carly standing at their campfire circle. She had her little girl with her, and they both had their hands full of pans and dishes.

"I'll try again," Rosie vowed to herself.

"Hello, Rosie. I'd like to start with an apology," Carly said with a smile. "We've brought dinner. A peace offering."

Rosie looked down quickly. In spite of her vow to try again, she'd already let resentment build behind her eyes, and was pretty sure some of it was leaking out. She raised her face to Carly after a second.

"We all do need to eat, that's for sure," Rosie conceded. "And, listen, I was a bitch earlier. It's me who should be apologizing."

They stood facing each other for a few seconds before DD made a little grunt of impatience. "Mama, this stuff is heavy," she complained. "Can I set it down?"

"We need to see where Rosie wants us to put it first," Carly replied. "That is, if you want it, Rosie?"

Rosie turned abruptly and began to clear off the small camp table that sat just outside the circle of logs around the fire.

"Set it all here, girls. I'm really touched that you'd bring food out to us. Like I said, I was in a bitchy mood this morning and treated you way worse than I should have."

Carly and DD put down their burdens on the table. Carly had brought a pan full of bacon on a paper towel, with lettuce leaves and huge tomato slices at the other end of the pan. Plain white bread slices sat vertically in the center of the pan, separating the bacon from the vegetables. DD had plates and knives and mustard and a jar of mayonnaise arranged in a box.

"We've brought the fixings for BLT sandwiches," Carly announced. "You know how to make those?"

"Oh, yeah, we know BLTs," Rosie laughed. "It's kinda hard to live in farm country without learning that delicacy."

"I kind of figured you'd like it," Carly chuckled back. "DD, do you want to go to the house and get some napkins or paper towels, please? I can't believe I forgot them."

Carly had deliberately left them, though, because she needed a minute or two alone with Rosie. She'd give it another honest try; surely they could work together for the good of the kids, if not for each other. Rosie had the same thought, but hadn't had a chance to invite DD to go look at the tents.

Thus similarly aligned, Carly and Rosie sat on log stumps right next to each other and took stock.

"How long have you lived out here, Carly?" Rosie began.

"We've lived out here for almost 10 years. DD is eight, and we moved here two years before that. How long have you been with Alaine?"

Rosie looked a little put off that Carly had turned her interview back to Rosie's situation, but took the detour with grace.

"I met Alaine six years ago in a café in Chicago. It's a long story and not very original. Unimpressive, I'd say, as far as amazing mothers go. I'll tell you the whole thing someday."

"Do you think we could be allies out here," Carly asked hesitantly. "It's just that—" She waved her hand slowly around at the farm.

"It's just that what? You didn't ask for an invasion of some guy with a woman and kids?" Rosie said with a smile, to take the sting out of the comment.

Carly laughed ruefully, low in her throat. Shook her head. "I didn't ask for that, true, but there's a whole raft of heartache that I didn't ask for, either," Carly murmured. "I could sure use some help with that."

"Let me guess. A long story? You'll tell me sometime?"

"You got it," Carly said. "It's not that I want to lead with that, though. I really don't. But when I think about what our dreams were when we moved out here and what we're faced with now…"

"It's not what you wanted for yourself?" Rosie asked. "I only say that because I'm right there with ya."

DD came skipping back to the camp with both napkins and a paper towel roll.

"I brought both cuz I couldn't remember which you wanted," she said cautiously.

"That's perfect, little one," Carly smiled. "I guess we should holler at the guys and see if they want to eat. What do you think, Rosie?"

"I think that's a great idea. Let's get them together."

The three made sure the food was covered and walked out to where the men were working on either fencing or cabin-staking. Mitchell, Alaine, Pike, and Trout all stood up in a line when the women approached.

"Who's hungry?" Rosie announced.

CHAPTER FIFTEEN

After the cabins were built, and the summer had passed, all seven of them had taken to gathering in the front room of the original farmhouse. They called it "visiting time." It had started as a way to learn more about each other; there was an old straw broom, useless as a cleaning implement, that they used as the "speaking broom." They'd take turns passing it around, and when one of them had something to say, they would gesture for the broom and tell their thing only after they held the broom in their hand. Pike tended to talk about fish that he caught; he'd spend far too much time on the killing and gutting of it, but that's how he was built. Trout would rarely ask for the broom. When he did, he'd tell of the progress of the wild cattails along the bank, or seeing tadpoles turning into frogs. DD never said anything, even when the broom passed to her. She'd smile shyly and pass it along. Mitchell occasionally said something about the crops or the garden or some chore he'd completed, but it wasn't ever remarkable.

The situation became complicated when Alaine kept calling for the broom. Even when Rosie or Carly put their hand up to speak, he would put his palm out like a traffic cop and would say, "Yes, of course, you two can speak. I just need to complete this thought and then I will pass the broom." The problem was he never did complete a thought. One thought led to another and he rarely bothered with transition sentences or checking faces to see if anyone had a response.

It got so Rosie gave up; she'd seen this hyper-focus before in Doyle. And resigned herself to it again with Alaine. Carly sat in frustration for a few weeks of sessions before she gave up, too. By the time the leaves of the cottonwood had turned golden and a few of them had dropped, they all knew that when Alaine called a "visiting time" it was going to be a long, boring sermon while Alaine impressed himself with his words.

"We should call this place the Compound," he declared in one typical gathering. "The Kingdom Compound of the Counsel of Prophecy. I've had a word from the Lord overnight. In a dream. The most *powerful* kind of dream; the one where an angel visits and brings a joy of rightness and purpose. Let me tell you all about it," Alaine said, and proceeded to unfurl a 20-minute story of the Word that the Angel had brought to him.

Carly suffered most of his speaking in silence, only shifting back and forth when Alaine started to speak about the way he thought all women in general, but specifically his woman—as he characterized Rosie— needed to stop what she was doing and meet his demands when they arose, be they for food, or rest, or clothes, or her sacred duty. Carly didn't feel like sex was an appropriate subject to discuss, especially when there were three children in the room. She'd asked Mitchell about it one evening.

"Do you think it's creepy that he tells us about having sex with Rosie?"

"I don't, actually, Mitchell replied. "He and I talked about that. I wish you would hear him better, and think of my needs more often."

"Wait. Are you saying you discuss our sex life with Alaine?"

"Of course. He counsels me," Mitchell said. "Carly, he has a direct line of communication to the Lord. Of *course* I'm going to listen to him!"

"That's just sick. Our bedroom is none of his business."

"Well, there's where you're wrong. I've been trying to hint at this for a while now, but since you brought it up, I need you to follow my dictates better. I'm asking you to be obedient unto me in the ways of the flesh."

"You could at least *try* some romance, Mitchell," she scoffed. "And since when do you talk like the Old Testament?"

For her part, Doug David was sick of the "threads of harmony," which Alaine kept returning to in their visiting time. Alaine twitched his fingers every time he used the phrase, first of all. Second, the "threads" were really all and only rules for behavior. While the threads of harmony may have started out as a pure and holy way to feel if a person was within the Will of God, Mitchell was the only adult still in the thrall of Alaine's self-centered worldview.

More than once Carly wished she could talk Mitchell out of the fanboy worship that he had for Alaine. When she tried, though, to break through to Mitchell, he'd get defensive and angry, and Carly would see his fists clench. That's when she'd back off because, coincidence or not, Mitchell's anger had gotten much less toxic ever since Alaine had shown up on the farm.

CHAPTER SIXTEEN

When DD was 15, Pike was 18, and Trout was 17, the new normal at the farm had Alaine as the spiritual leader. Rosie continued to slog along as a subservient partner and mother, trapped in her worry about being found by Doyle. Carly had given up griping to Mitchell about asking Alaine to leave, and Mitchell continued to appreciate the direction and leadership that he absorbed from Alaine.

"Doug David, come here for a moment," Alaine demanded one afternoon.

She looked up from her planting, her legs still spread wide while she burrowed potato pieces into the hills they'd mounded. She turned to see him behind her, standing at the end of the row. She laid her small trowel down next to the tin bucket of potato eyes, turning towards him, and slapping the dirt off her hands.

"Yes, sir," she said, resigned to another lecture.

She hadn't had much one-on-one interaction with him since he'd moved onto their property nine years ago. She kept her head down and tried to stay out of Alaine's way. Her time had been spent learning Bible verses from Rosie, learning to sew, learning to cook, and sitting for visiting time, broom and all, while Alaine spoke to them.

"You've grown into a beautiful young woman, Doug David." He was using his persuader voice. The one he used in the evening when he was trying to convince them all that he was right and knew a truth that they didn't understand yet.

This attention he gave to her was new. His long beard hid the planes of his face, but his eyes crinkled as he watched her watching him. It felt nothing like the wave of emotion she got when she was looked at by Trout.

"Thank you, Alaine. I had nothing to do with that," she said.

"Haha, yes, that's true! The Good Lord saw fit to grow you into beauty, didn't he?"

"If you say so." She was curt, wishing the conversation to be over.

"I do. And, someday, you and I need to honor God's plan by pursuing a deeper understanding of that beauty," he proclaimed, lifting his hands as if he had orchestrated her maturing. "Do you agree?"

"I guess so," she said, although she didn't quite know what that meant.

"I will Call for you when the Lord tells me to. I hope you will trust my Understanding at that time."

He looked at her meaningfully, one eye half-closed in an almost-wink, and held her gaze until she dipped her chin. She restrained herself from shuddering, but only just. She waited until Alaine had walked into the house before she bent over in the rows to finish her task.

A week after that encounter in the potatoes, DD went to find her mother. Carly sat in the farmhouse working on both a sourdough starter and doing some mending. When Doug David came in, Carly gave her a sunny smile until she saw the profound agitation on her face. She realized then how grown up her daughter had become, passing into womanhood too quickly for Carly's comfort level.

"What's wrong?" Carly asked.

"Mother, is this place, this arrangement, healthy?"

"What do you mean?" Carly said with alarm.

DD pursed her lips and said carefully, "I mean, do you think—you, I mean, not Alaine—this is a normal group of people living together?"

"Why do you ask that? What's happened?" Carly's voice rose in pitch.

"It's just that... I don't know anything past this farm, and I don't have anything to compare it to," DD admitted, "so I could be way off."

"Compare what to?" Carly's stood up from the table, her face reddening.

"It's just that, I'm having trouble understanding what my role is, now that I'm a woman," DD puzzled out.

"Who said you are a woman?" Carly asked sternly. She placed her hands on the table top and leaned forward.

"Alaine did. A week ago. When I was planting potatoes."

"A week ago! Honey, he has no right to decide that! I had no idea. You should have come straight to me! You don't have a *role*, you're our daughter. You are an original resident. We three don't have *roles*, we have ownership. And we say who stays and who goes," Carly ended with menace.

Doug David looked at her doubtfully, wondering if her mother believed that or was just trying to convince her that the living situation had not gone off course.

"Do you really believe that? That you and daddy are still in charge?" she asked carefully.

DD could tell that her mother was furious. What she couldn't tell is if she was furious at her. Or someone else.

"Of course we're in charge! Just the other day, your father told Alaine that he didn't want another building put up as a solitary home."

"You mean like that one they're working on right now?" Doug David motioned out the window to the framed building already half finished.

Carly rubbed her forehead. "I guess your father lost that argument."

"I think it's bad here," Doug David declared. "It's gotten worse, but really slowly. Like I said, I'm just a kid who's never seen anything work or not work. But this," she swept her hand as if across the expanse of the farm, "this doesn't feel like it's working anymore."

"You may be right, little one. You may be absolutely right." Carly sat back down at the table with a worried look on her face. "I better do something about that."

CHAPTER SEVENTEEN

During this time of farm—Compound—expansion, Doug David realized she had a preference between the brothers. Pike almost always found a way to dig at her, or insult her outright, or put a roadblock in the way of whatever chore she'd been assigned that day. He would hide the hoe or the shovel, so she'd have to walk all the way to the barn to get a different one for the garden. When she got back from the barn, the hoe would be leaning against the house where she thought she'd left it all along. At first, she thought it was her own forgetfulness, but she'd taken to watching out the window, through the slit in the curtains. Pike would sidle up to the house, look left and right, and take the hoe, or the shovel, or the barrow, and move it over behind his own sleeping cabin. She'd make the walk to the barn, then watch him, through the barn door, return whatever implement she needed in the first place.

Trout, on the other hand, tended to draw an authentic smile from deep within her whenever she saw him. If he was alone—away from Pike, that is—she allowed the smile to reach her face and shine with full wattage right at him so he couldn't miss it. Trout would take five minutes to help her with whatever chore she was doing. He didn't mind hanging sheets, for instance, even if that was "part of the women's work of harmony," as Alaine called it. The one flaw to their subtle dance was that if Pike was with him, or even if he was present, Trout would settle for being just a touch kinder than Pike was. Which was a pretty low bar.

"Been to see your baby tree yet, Dougie?" Pike would sneer.

Trout would glare at him, sometimes slug him, but they never outright battled over Pike's treatment of Doug David. At best, Trout would hurry them along so the conflict was over soon. Doug David had stopped answering Pike long ago, realizing that made him angrier than any retort she could quickly come up with.

Doug David sat in what she'd taken to calling her "inland chapel," the space between the junipers that her mother had shown her long ago. It had taken a back seat to the space she liked to sit in right alongside the river, but this was still her own. The two boys, problematic in different ways, hadn't yet found her while she sat here. She'd come to the realization that she wanted Trout to find her as badly as she wanted Pike to never show up in her life again.

"There's something off about him," she murmured. "He's a right trial, that's for sure."

Around the time Alaine had given her the speech in the potato rows, her daydreams had switched from prairie flowers and lazy hawks shadowing the grass to Trout running his hands along her arms and smiling at her. Every time they passed, she felt a swell of joy and peace, plus her body had started to tingle for the few minutes after, while the feeling lingered. She'd been meaning to talk to her mama about it, but hadn't. She doubted her mother would do anything helpful about this, either. She'd still said nothing to Alaine about the potato patch incident.

"It's just that mama never brings up anything about attraction or love or whether it's right or wrong," she said aloud to herself. "So how am I supposed to know?"

Doug David picked up the berries that had fallen off the tree until she had a small handful. She rubbed the lighter, frosted blue color off all of them. She flicked them, one by one, at the anthill at the edge of the glade. The ants didn't notice or care; they had work to do, after all, and the vagaries of the planet had no more impact on their toil than did a few juniper berries cast at them, raining down from above. Doug David sat watching them, noticing that only one of the berries got close to an ant trail, and the ants just detoured around it. She wondered if there was a message for her in that. *Detour, sure, but from what?*

❖

One shining fall afternoon that same year she was 15, Doug David had walked to the bank of the Ninnescah and settled in some deep prairie grass that ran right up to the water's edge. She knew from past experience that the place was invisible to every other building on the farm, so she could truly relax and enjoy the day.

Carp sucked cottonwood seeds, drifted down from their parent trees, from the surface of the water in eddies near the bank. She watched the swirl of the water where cotton and leaves circled, and watched the three or four carp nudge up to the surface, tasting it all to see what they liked. A hawk floated above in wide circles. She stretched her legs out, set her hands on her lap, smiled at the day.

"I love this place," she heard someone say.

She tried not to scream, and tried not to jump straight up. She managed to hold the scream to a strangled cough, and shifted her legs to cover her alarm.

"Don't be scared, Doug David. I didn't mean to startle you," Trout said.

"How'd you get here without me hearing you?"

"I was already here. Laying down. Truth is, I mighta dropped off for a second there. But when you didn't notice me, I wasn't sure what to do."

"Oof! Well, silly me, I guess. I was so glad for a second to myself, I didn't look around. Also, I've never showed this place to anyone."

"It's not a huge Compound, Doug David. I know all about this place. Got several other prime spots to rest, too, for that matter."

"We're never really alone, are we?" she mused.

"Not like I'd like to be. With you," he said quietly.

She looked over at Trout, who had propped himself on one elbow. His head was still low in the grass, and several stalks of bluestem split her view of his face. She drew her knees up and wrapped her arms around them. She put a piece of her hair in her mouth, sucked on it, then exchanged it for a piece of bluestem.

Trout looked at her mouth where the grass sat. "Lucky grass," he said.

"You want a piece?" A heat rising up her neck and into her cheeks.

"I'd take that piece, if you're offering."

For a season, she'd thought her awareness of where Trout was on the farm, her need to know what he was doing, was just part of being a responsible community member. She realized, with a rush of heat, that he felt something towards her same as she did for him.

"Are you saying you want to suck on the same piece of grass that I sucked on?"

"I'm saying, uh, that I wish I could touch your lips, like that grass did," he said, his own face reddening.

"I doubt that's in keeping with our *rules of behavior.*"

"I don't care about those. I care about you."

"Do you?"

"I do. I hardly get anything done, at least, not as fast as I could." He grinned. "I'm always walking past you to see what you are doing."

"And here I thought you were just practicing helpfulness," she laughed.

"Oh, it's helpful, all right. To my sanity."

She leaned towards him, putting her right arm down on the ground. He moved towards her, too. Their faces drew close, two sets of lips meeting, moving, exploring. The tip of her tongue slipped out and flicked his teeth, surprising them both. They drew apart, breathing hard, eyes shining.

The dinner bell rang in the distance. Trout motioned her to stay where she was, and he jumped to his feet to run back to the main house. As he turned, she noticed his trousers bunching oddly. She flung herself backwards on the ground, full length, stretching luxuriously in this new feeling. Like a sun had sprung into new life inside of her, burning away everything that had been in shadow. After a minute, she stood, brushed her skirt smooth, and walked, shoulders back, towards dinner.

Helping her mother make the meal, Doug David let her mind wander back to that moment on the banks of the creek. Even as she dipped the chicken into the dredge, the seasoning, and then laid the pieces in the cast iron skillet, her face had a half-smile on it. She mashed the potatoes with an easy grace, putting a big wooden spoon in the bowl before she set in on the table. As the other six trooped into the dining room, she straightened her spine and set her face in a bland expression, smiling at each person as they sat. She loved a good fried chicken dinner, even though it took a lot of work. She especially loved preparing food for Trout, who now occupied almost every waking moment of her brain. She'd keep an eye on him while he ate, enjoying his appetite, and thinking about his lips.

CHAPTER EIGHTEEN

Pike was not blind. He knew something had kindled in Trout, whom he shared a room with, and it didn't take a genius—which Pike wasn't—to put Doug David on the short list of "things that have changed." Part of what the men talked about when they had their "men's sessions" was the state of the women on the Compound. Alaine had declared Doug David a "woman" last summer, when she'd started walking taller, lost much of the timidity that often goes hand in hand with girlhood, and grew into her curves. Alaine told them there's never an exact time that a girl becomes a woman, but he knew it when he saw it. As the spiritual leader of the Compound, he got only token resistance from Mitchell.

"She's my daughter, Alaine. I won't have her listed like this, as an *asset*," Mitchell objected.

"Mitchell, womanhood is one of the marvels of God's Plan, and who are we to thwart Him?" Alaine responded. "Not adding her would be like trying to deny the moon's phases. That's all there is to it. It doesn't mean anything; she won't be used as a Vessel until she agrees to it, and until you and Carly agree to it. You have my Word."

"I'll hold you to that, leader or not," Mitchell said, in a protective, restrained—barely—voice of a father.

"I keep my Word, do I not?"

A quick flash across Mitchell's face—a deep gray thundercloud—showed his anger. But just for a second. "You'd better."

Pike considered several times if he should accuse Trout of having—well, something—with DD. He wasn't smart enough to figure out how to accuse Trout of loving DD, though, and Pike couldn't puzzle out a way to point a finger without Alaine telling him to stop gossiping.

Alaine watched Pike tussle with the relationship. He watched Trout and DD fall for each other. He smiled to himself when Mitchell and Carly stayed oblivious. Alaine decided the situation would serve his continued dominance. It would serve just fine.

It turned late March by the time the chunks of ice that clogged the river broke apart enough to flow, then soften, then melt. Doug David had waited impatiently for the season to let go, and waited with even more anticipation for the spring shoots to show themselves. Everyone on the farm, in her opinion, had gone a little cabin-bound while they waited for the icy mud to dry into the firm dirt tracks they used to travel between buildings. When they were all cooped up together, as loving as it was, there was no time to steal glances, let alone words, with the axis around whom she spun these days: Trout.

Trout watched her just as carefully, though he was overly dismissive if they ever had to share a task, or if they sat next to each other at the meal or at the service. Pike lurked in the background, judging each of their performances, testing Trout every night with his sarcastic and ribald comments. He knew that Pike knew, but he was surprised that no one else commented on his infatuation that, he thought, was emblazoned all over his face every time he got near her. Like two halves of fissionable material glowing as the scientist moved them closer together; like a magnet that slowly bearded itself with tiny iron filings.

A warm spring wind, from the south, pushed Doug David as she walked to her spot by the river. She paused a moment at the roots of the cottonwood, remembering her never-known brothers. She thought about her mother, how faithful she was, how careful she was to always love Doug David, and how deliberate she was to never ask Doug David to live up to the legacy of her tiny, unrealized brothers. She walked on, wondering if her father ever came to this place.

She sat. The ground beneath her was cold, and a little damp. Her skirt drew moisture from the dirt, but it wasn't uncomfortable enough to shift away or give up. The bluestem still stood tall, but it was last year's growth, and this was sparse and rattling in the breeze. Almost half an hour passed; most of her break time from tilling the garden to prep for planting of peas and asparagus.

In a rush, Trout flopped to the ground next to her, laughing at her surprise. "I had to run over here—Pike was watching every move I made!" he said. "I finally got dad to call him over to help inspect the cabin joints for cracking, but only because I said, out loud, that Pike hadn't tried very hard last fall."

"He'll be mad about that, won't he?"

"He's always mad about something. It never matters, anyway. He's frustrated all the time these days," Trout lamented.

"I don't want him to hurt you, is all," DD said intimately.

"He's all talk, no do. I'll be fine."

They stopped talking and lunged toward each other. They hadn't touched, hardly, except by accident on purpose, during the entire winter. Their hunger for each other's touch had grown; had outstripped the new spring growth underneath them. Had arrived in a blaze of fire that ignites kindling laid for a fire, protected from damp.

"Oh, man! I'm—" Trout started.

He didn't finish his sentence. Not with words, anyway. They clutched each other, neither able to think straight.

"I feel the same way," she laughed as their mouths stayed open to each other.

In their purity of heart, they kissed and considered that enough. As they continued, though, spots on each of their bodies grew hot enough to demand, in a primal sense, satisfaction. She tentatively put her hand on his leg, right at the bend between thigh and pelvis. She felt his pulse through her palm, pushed back against it in rhythm. He wrapped his hand around her ribcage, lower than her breasts. She arched her back towards his hand, and flicked her tongue again at his; two swords in riposte.

They broke apart, again breathing heavily, picking up right where they left off last fall.

"I think we are in big trouble, Trout," she said, her chest heaving as if she'd run a mile.

"If this is trouble, then I want more," he said. "Meet me tomorrow. Not here. I'll tell you where after supper when you are doing dishes. OK?"

"I'll do that."

She got up, brushed her skirt again, and flapped it around a little so the damp spot from the spring moisture wouldn't be so obvious. If anyone cared, that is. She walked back to the garden spot, picked up the three-tined tool, and swung happily at every clod of dirt that she saw.

After supper, in the line of women washing and drying dishes, she heard Trout telling a loud joke about eating hedge apples over by the pig barn. When she glanced his way, he winked at her just as he delivered the punch line to the men who sat in the living room, "...and *that's* the last time I trusted a *pig* to tell me about *apples*!" he said as the men all cracked up. Doug David hadn't heard the setup to the joke, but it didn't make sense to her. Pigs couldn't talk, after all. But the message was loud and clear: pig barn under the hedge of Osage orange trees.

When she got to the hedgerow the next afternoon, Trout was already there. He'd spread an old quilt on the ground, and he'd picked a scraggly bouquet of early wildflowers that he handed to her as she twisted down to sit.

"It's all I could find that bloomed," he said sheepishly. "Sorry."

She took the flowers, pulled one out, threaded it behind her ear. "I love them. Thank you, Trout."

"This feels like Song of Solomon, Doug David."

"How so?"

"You are the orchard. I'm the farmer, or the fox, I forget which. I never was supposed to read much of that book, dad always said."

"I'm fruit, you mean?"

He gently reached a hand to her breast, clumsy at her buttoned blouse. He made steady progress, though, and gave her ample time to stop him. Her eyes shone as she let him continue and as she slid her thumbs underneath his suspenders off his shoulders. Moved her own fingers to his buttons, moving quicker now, both of them succumbing to gravity as they lay sideways next to each other. They answered the insistent calls of each of those hot spots within themselves and each other, clasping their arms tightly around the other in a way that only two who shall become one could understand.

Afterward, the breeze drying their sweat, they kissed each other with bruised and puffy lips, murmuring how wonderful they felt, how right it was. Youth being youth, one thing led to another, and they again shared the bliss that they'd recently discovered before dressing hurriedly and scampering off, separately, to finish the afternoon chores they'd each been assigned.

When they'd left, Pike slid down the roof of the pig barn, having watched the performance from above. He knelt in the trampled grass where the two had lain, smelling them still, wishing it was he.

Not long after that spring day, Pike cornered Doug David in the gardening shed. He was agitated and breathing heavily. She had returned the remaining onion sets to the shed, and was putting them back on the shelf along the rear wall and covering them with sand. He slammed the door behind him, leaning a short shovel against the door so it wouldn't open from the outside.

"I want what Trout got," he demanded.

Pike approached her quickly, reaching his arms out to pin her own arms to her side. He pushed his scraggly-bearded face into her neck, breathing heavily, obscenely, to try and smell her. He didn't wash often and he smelled like a farm animal. Doug David struggled against his arms that were strong bands of gristle but made no progress in freeing herself.

"Pike! Stop it!"

"I'll stop when I'm good and ready," he moaned.

She brought her knee up. Right into his crotch. Although her skirt slowed the impact, it was still hard enough to cause him to let go, hunch over, and drop to the floor with his hands grasping his wounded balls. She tried to step past him, and he rallied enough to grab her ankle. He pulled. She dropped to the floor, where they lay head to toe. He scrabbled to sit up, then he pulled her around so her head was near his lap.

"It's not fair that he gets you and I don't!" he shouted.

"I'm not a thing to share! You don't have a right!" she yelled back.

"Keep your voice down, or else," he hissed.

"Or else *what?* You'll hurt me? Too late for threats, you idiot."

"I want you to shut up and let me."

"I'll let you do *nothing.* You get *nothing!*" she roared as she kicked her foot at him.

To this point, Doug David had suffered as a "lesser being" and "in need of direction" because that was the message Alaine droned on about day after day and week after week. Her father had somehow come under Alaine's spell and used many subtle ways of approving that message of submission. Today, though, she'd had enough. Perhaps it was because this was the first time her personal space had been violated. Perhaps it was because she now understood what a man could take from her. Coming so soon after she offered the very same thing to Trout, the violation showed even more starkly across the landscape of her liberty.

Her foot caught him on his chin. His eyes glazed, and she saw a tooth driven through his tongue and sticking out its bottom. Blood spurted from his mouth then ran steadily as he laid back against the dirt flooring of the shed. He'd let go of her. She rose to her feet, eyes in a blaze of fury, stopped herself from kicking him, over and over.

Doug David moved the shovel that had blocked the door and walked out of the shed. She stepped around the far side of it to collect herself, put her hair back in order, and check her clothes for blood.

"If that's the end of it I'll be shocked," she murmured to herself. "But I'll be damned if I'm the one that brings it up first."

She walked back to the garden and stood there, at a total loss as to why she'd gone to the shed in the first place. She went to find her mother.

Part 4

THE UNRAVELING

CHAPTER NINETEEN

"Don't ask me to come talk to you in the glade about this, DD," Carly hissed at her in the kitchen. "It's not up for discussion! Those boys are trouble and always have been. You stay away. And if you haven't stayed away, get yourself away!"

"Mother, I'm asking you to come to the glade. I need advice about Trout. It can't always be a lecture in the kitchen!"

"Not this time, DD. Not this time!" Carly yelled.

DD stumbled out of the house and wandered. Her mother's rejection stung; the biggest sting of all was the absence of her mama's "little one" endearment. DD wondered when her mother had quit thinking of her daughter as "little one." She realized she hadn't heard it for a long time—too long.

Carly listened to DD storm off, knowing that they owed each other a real conversation someday, but hoping she still had time to finesse the malfunctions happening with Mitchell, with Rosie, with Alaine.

Alaine, after Pike's violation, saw it all slipping away. All those years ago—was it seven or eight now?—

when he planted his feet and claimed the land for his own. Just like the Old Testament—now *there* were some leaders!—when they could stand on a space, or in a river, or a town square and call it their own. Dare anyone to come deny their claim. He could feel his Kingdom Prophecy Compound crumbling like the walls of Jericho. This was to be his crowning glory, his magnum opus, his life's work.

"Though I am but a humble Servant, surely I am the more Holy, and My claim should be the one you Honor!" he shouted.

There comes a time when a narcissist is found out and they scrabble for better footing or a spin that returns them to authority. A moment where the dice have been cast and he comes up a loser. He felt that sick sense of loss right now, even though the Compound was still under his control, the adults were whipped dogs and he held the whip, and the boys still didn't realize that they had agency of their own to make decisions that didn't include pleasing Alaine.

Alaine approached Carly while she was prepping vegetables in the farmhouse kitchen.

"Carly, hello."

"Alaine." She did not stop moving her hands with the peeler. She did not make eye contact.

"I'd sit and speak with you for a while, if I may." He didn't ask so much as assert. It had been some time since he felt he needed anyone's permission for any of his actions.

"As you wish. I'll keep working."

"Of course. You're a dutiful wife. Ever since the day I made the pact with Mitchell and you raised nary a scrap of protest."

He looked at her, appraisingly. She glanced at him, but furtively, not wanting him to suspect her of disloyalty.

"I wondered then. I wonder even more now," he mused, one side of his face raised in a question.

He waited her out.

"What did you wonder, Alaine?" she finally asked.

"Is it difficult?"

"Is what difficult?"

"Is it difficult for you. To stay faithful. And to deny yourself."

"I have no idea what you're talking about, Alaine." She continued with the food on the counter, her face a mask.

"Oh, I think you do." He shifted his legs, pushed himself away from the table, and turned the chair to face her directly.

Carly's forehead compressed and her lips drained of blood as she pressed them to each other and against her teeth. She breathed heavily through her nose. She pushed at a lock of hair that had come loose and hung in her vision.

"See?" he said. "That is what I mean. Your body is betraying you, my dear Carly. You've not been complete. Not been completed. I regret that I did not recognize your desire for me sooner. We could have made a Child of God together."

"Desire?" she shouted. "Ha!"

He chuckled. Almost a croak. He stretched his hands out to her, softened his face. "Come. You need not deny yourself any longer, Carly. You are as Ruth was, laying at my feet, delivering yourself to me," he intoned. "I've been blind, Lord! Yet now I see," he breathed.

He stood and moved towards her, implacable and inevitable. She turned back to the counter and tried to leave the kitchen, but he pressed against her. She could feel him—his arousal—and nausea flooded her senses. Her mouth filled with saliva. She gripped the potato peeler tightly, turned into him, put the point at his ribs.

"Ah, yes, I knew you felt the same!" he said. "And, yes, I *feel* your torment. Did not Christ himself suffer a pierced side?"

"Get *off* me! Get *away* from me! Mitchell!" she yelled. Carly pushed the point of the kitchen gadget into him, but did not truly believe she needed to hurt him. If only she had.

"Let yourself go, Carly. Let this happen, if not now, then later," he breathed into her neck.

"No! Get away!"

They heard the screen door spring and the wooden door slam against the wall. Alaine stepped back hurriedly, Mitchell entering with fire in his eyes. Alaine saw the opportunity and took it.

"Carly," Alaine thundered. "I have told you, time and time again, I am not for you!"

"Mitchell," Carly cried. "He attacked me!"

"What do you two think you're doing?" Mitchell roared.

All three spoke at the same time. All three heaved breath as if they'd run to the point of exhaustion. Alaine recognized that every second favored him. He turned to Mitchell with his look of *weary leader* to make his case.

"Mitchell, my friend. My *brother*. I have tried to deny that this was happening. I've told her for *years* that I could not break our bond. The bond we made on the porch those many years ago."

"Mitchell! Do *not* listen to him! He's gone mad. I would *never*," Carly hissed.

Carly was so angry she was crying. Mitchell's face had gotten even redder than when he came in. He deliberately set the spade he'd been carrying in the corner of the kitchen, small clods of dirt sliding down to the floor.

"I'll leave you two alone," Alaine said. "I believe you have a need for conversation. One that I should not be privy to." He quickly strode across the room and pushed outside through the screen door. He clomped loudly across the porch the steps. Then quietly crept back to the side of the screen door to listen, the barest grin etching his face.

Inside, Carly took a step towards Mitchell. "You've got to know that he is insane."

"Do I, Carly?"

"Mitchell!"

"Carly!" he replied in the same tone.

"There is no way—in no universe—that what he said is true!"

"I've always wondered, though," Mitchell sneered.

"This is a control move! Not a real thing, Mitchell," she pleaded. "You've got to see that!"

"All I see is you looking as alive and wild as I remember you used to be," he said. "Like you never are with me. Anymore."

"That isn't arousal, Mitchell, it's fear—he was forcing himself on me! I spread my legs for you whenever you ask! Don't you dare accuse me of wanting him!"

"Like a chore, sure. Do you like it? I kinda doubt it."

He was still yelling. She was still yelling. She threw the peeler in the sink, let out a scream of rage. He picked up the chair and smashed it on the floor. Shook the remaining piece at her while he screamed right back. Primal rage, barely restrained from both of them. Mitchell turned to the door, grabbed the shovel, stomped out onto the porch. Carly put both hands on the counter, crying and trembling.

Alaine had heard it all. He dashed off the porch and a few feet into the yard before Mitchell's exit and listened for the door to swing open. Alaine abruptly turned back to the house, looking as if he was returning.

"Mitchell—how did it go?" he oozed.

"I can't talk right now, Alaine! I'm furious!" Mitchell barked.

Mitchell stalked towards the river. Alaine trailed him by only a step. It took hardly any time to get to the river bank, where Mitchell drove the spade into the sandy soil.

"Tell me! Tell me why you are furious, Mitchell," Alaine soothed.

"I'm furious because I can't tell who is lying to me!" Mitchell screamed.

Alaine smiled to himself. The battle was over; he just needed to get Mitchell to see it. "Yes, that's right," Alaine encouraged. "Speak your fury! The Lord wants to hear your truth. He sent me to Hear your truth. And to speak His Truth back to you."

"I can't hear a sermon right now, Alaine," Mitchell shot back. "I'm sorry. With respect, I mean."

"Of course. A man's raw anger does not need apology, my brother. A man's righteous fury when he is Wronged is always—always—a duty to speak," Alaine intoned.

Mitchell stood at the riverbank. He shook with the adrenaline that coursed through his body. Sweat dripped off his face. He clasped and unclasped his hands, rendered speechless in his impotent rage.

Alaine stood next to him, hiding his own trembling—so close to disaster!—in order to look serene and sure in God's Plan. All for Mitchell's benefit. All for Alaine's own survival. "A deep breath, Mitchell. We have faced the faithless before, have we not? We can work around Carly. It's actually good to know where she stands, in a way. We know—you and I know—that we must guard ourselves."

Alaine laid a hand on Mitchell's shoulder, pressed his fingers into the rigid muscle. Patted him three times. Crossed his hands behind his back, once again secure in what he surveyed.

Carly had not been the first of her family to give birth to twins; she knew that. She immediately wondered about Doug David when it became clear she was pregnant, too. Carly had noticed her signs of early pregnancy and thought back to the time when DD asked for a meeting in the glade. *Oh, well, water under the bridge*, Carly thought.

Even though she knew she wasn't supposed to talk with her—her own daughter!—she still went in search of DD one afternoon. She found her in the garden again, tending the full potato plants so the yield would be as high as possible.

"Doug David, you're pregnant." An observation, not a question.

DD looked at her mother's face before she answered. It was easier to navigate the adults when she could match her words to the body posturing she saw.

"Hello, mother. Yes," she responded in the same tone.

"Is that what you wanted to tell me last week? Is Alaine the father? Or is it one of the boys?"

"Alaine?! Definitely not!"

"Pike or Trout, then?"

DD didn't answer. She held up two fingers, nodded her head to the right. She didn't have to say Trout's name because her face showed the truth of her and Trout's love.

Her mother's face had turned bleak, like when a sunny winter's day is overtaken by a squall of snow, ice, and plummeting temperatures. The kind of storm that drove people indoors as quickly as possible, and the kind of face that stopped Doug David, with her mouth half-open, from telling her mother how wonderful it was to spend time with Trout and that they wanted to spend a life together. Doug David saw all that cross her mother's face and settle into her body.

"Mother, let's go inside. I don't want to have this talk out in the open."

They went inside and into the kitchen, where they sat down.

"Well, it doesn't matter. You can't keep the babies. It's a rule of the Compound. A rule from the Lord," Carly said without pity.

"What in the world else would I do with them?" Doug David was incredulous.

"You don't get to keep them. Women who aren't married don't get to have babies," Carly recited from Alaine's threads.

"I'm clearly going to have a baby. So that rule isn't true," DD objected.

Carly surprised them both by standing and swinging her hand, full-armed, at Doug David's face.

"I'll thank you to be respectful, daughter," Carly shouted, the imprint of the hand reddening on DD's cheek.

"Mother, I—"

"Think carefully before you speak your next words, little one," Carly menaced.

"It's just that..." Doug David had a hard time beginning the words she wanted to say. "You didn't used to treat me like a problem," she finally said. "Not when it was just us," she added softly.

"*Just us* was years ago! I don't treat you like a *problem*," Carly objected. "You just don't like having the rules apply to you, too. Is that it?"

"I don't like being second place behind Alaine," DD snapped. "Since when did he get more important to you than me?"

Carly's spine grew even straighter. "You're not second place. You don't *have* a place. Your father set me straight on where we stand. And we stand in support of the greater good, which is serving the Lord," she said defensively.

Carly stood there, thinking about whether her comment was true. Mitchell had been furious when Carly asked him whether the farm was still a healthy place for them. He railed against the dangers of society, reminded her that they wanted to be left alone, and that Alaine had joined them at his invitation. The genesis of the complicated relationship that she and Mitchell had with Alaine was way back in her murky memory, so she didn't think, at first, that it was true.

Against her better judgment, seeing the pitiless stance of her mother, DD pleaded, "You used to hold my hand, mama. You used to let me smile at you for a long time, and you'd just smile back at me, not a care in the world. You didn't tell me all this 'I've got to do my chores for the good of the Compound' business. When did *that* take first place over me? Or over daddy, for that matter?"

It was another seminal moment for both of them. For Carly, who'd never seen her daughter as a woman-in-training, never realized she had actual opinions about her life, had never spoken of what she wished still existed, and, mostly, hadn't heard her daughter call her "mama" for a score of months.

For Doug David, it wasn't nearly as painful as she imagined it would be to tell her mother how she truly felt. She'd always thought it would be like a physical wound, where blood would flow and nerves would flare if she told either of her parents the truth. It felt nothing like pain; it was way more like those splinters her mother had pulled from her arms so long ago. Like levering a popcorn hull from behind a molar. A relief. Relief at returning to family. Only and solely family, without other people clouding her love or her mother's love. She sat down heavily at the table, spent like she'd run a mile.

"Doug David, I didn't realize. I thought you loved all this, but didn't like the woman part," Carly explained.

DD was taken aback for a moment at her mother's abrupt reversal of course. She sat for a moment before she spoke.

"Mama, I can tell that *you* love it, because you get the huge family that you always wanted. The many kids that you tried to have. That's a lot of pressure on me, ya know. To try and be those boys, too."

They both sat in silence after DD said that; a pool, rippling from the tossed stone.

"Oh, sweet child. I didn't mean to do that. *Any* of that. I just wanted—well, I don't know *what* I wanted. I'd bargained with God when the twins died. I've been tied by that ever since. And, I guess…" She paused. "I guess Alaine and his Word with the Lord and his Compound felt like an answer to my prayer. I prayed that for the night we buried the twins."

More silence. Their horizons changing at every revelation. Breath passing in and out.

"See? You've never told me that. I've *wondered* what his hold over you was."

"But if we had it to do over? I'd be more bossy and tell your father we didn't want to do that," Carly admitted.

"Tell your father you didn't want to do what?" Mitchell asked.

Arriving at the house and hearing them through the open window, he had stood and listened to his wife and daughter talking. Their subject was, to him, bedrock truth and not up for negotiation. He'd thrown his lot in with Alaine, that day on the porch, and never looked back. At Carly's spoken admission, he had stomped into the room.

Carly and DD looked startled at first, then quickly covered their alarm by smiling at him.

"Hi, daddy. Uh, I guess I've got news." Doug David rubbed her slightly pooching belly, a tiny, rueful smile on her face. She looked away from him, turning to her mother for reassurance. Both smiles got even wider, if that was possible; a hint of frantic to both of their faces.

"You are going to be a grandfather!" Carly exclaimed. "Isn't that great?"

Mitchell's face was overtaken by storm clouds. When Carly saw his face darken, it was all she could see and it took her back. To the bad days after they buried the twins.

Carly continued, "And what we were talking about was how unhappy she is with the living arrangements here on the Compound."

"Unhappy? Grandfather?" he shouted. "Start over, please!"

He'd spoken the last with ill grace, his voice rising to anger.

"Now, Mitchell, don't get how... you get," Carly begged. "Please just listen."

"Don't' tell me how I get!" Mitchell groused. "This best not be a re-hash of what I had to set you straight about the other day! I'd better sit down."

They passed back outside, through the garden fence, and onto the back porch. Doug David and Carly sat in the wicker loveseat, and Mitchell in the wicker chair at right angles to them. The matching glass table had a tin can with old flowers in it, and the water had evaporated in the bottom of the can. The stems of the flowers gave off a slightly rotting smell, which trickled past them on the light breeze.

"Daddy. I'm having a baby. It's ok. It's Trout. It has been for a while now," Doug David said simply.

"You've been having sex with Trout?" Mitchell yelled.

Carly laid a hand over near Mitchell. He quieted, but still fidgeted, his mouth working.

"Yes," DD said with a quiet confidence.

"You can't keep the babies," he said flatly.

"That's what mother told me, too." Doug David remained calm. "I'd like to know why not?"

"It's a rule, that's why. 'Women who are unmarried shall not keep the fruit of their sin.' That's the rule," Mitchell insisted.

Carly's face was a picture of grief. She only just now saw the terrible inhumanity and subjugation of all the females on the Compound, and her grief was worse that she'd been blind to it up to that point.

Doug David stood her ground. "I don't accept that rule, father. I'm pregnant, which makes me a future mother, which means I get to say what happens to my children. No one else."

"No! You are subject to the rules of the Compound," Mitchell declared.

"I ask a*gain.* Why?"

"That's the way it is. The Lord gave the rules to Alaine. We follow them," MItchell recounted. What he didn't say was that it was *easier* when he didn't have to make the rules and Alaine could just tell him what was right and what was wrong and that Mitchell couldn't handle the pressure of all the *decisions.*

"I'm keeping the baby," Doug David said without wavering. "It's fine if you want to follow the rules that Alaine has said he heard from God, but I'm not following that one. Mine. A gift and a promise *to me.* From God, who talks to me, too."

"You'll not!" Mitchell yelped. "I have no choice but to tell Alaine of your condition and make plans to re-home the baby, at such time as it is delivered." He turned to Carly. "And, frankly, I'd hoped you'd have figured out what she was doing with that miserable excuse for a boy and also make her see that she has no choice over her body when a man hasn't taken her properly as a husband."

"Mitchell, can you just wait a—" Carly pleaded.

But he'd already risen, tromped off the porch, and strode west towards Alaine's cabin. He didn't look back.

"Mama?" Doug David asked beseechingly.

They shared a look. Neither of them could find words of encouragement right away. DD because she'd always kept quiet and never played the role of encourager. Carly because she'd never realized how far afield she'd gotten from an independent young woman of hopes and dreams. The loss of her twins came roaring back into her spirit, sucking the energy and the life and the willpower from her.

"Well, we have a few months, don't we?" Carly said, trying to rally. "I mean, it looks like we have a few months. We just have to figure out a plan before your baby comes."

They collapsed into each other, relieved that they'd reconnected and could ally for each other. It was a close call as to which one of them cried harder; in the end, they both had damp hair and collars from their tears. Even after they quit crying, they sat quietly on the loveseat holding hands and watching the sunlight change the shadows across the farm.

The cottonwood stretched over both the river and the long grass. Doug David felt it reach towards her and give her strength. She gathered it and stored it and passed it onto the tiny little life she carried. She gripped her mother's hand tightly, too, passing the strength to her, feeling it come back to her from her mother, both of them changed; purified. A mother of a child. Two mothers. Carly knew, at that moment, she should leave quickly. Take Doug David by herself, if Mitchell didn't see reason. She had some money;

not nearly enough. Katie and Art had said 'anytime you need anything'—this surely qualified.

For the rest of that day, Carly knew she should leave when she finished hanging laundry, when she went into the kitchen to start supper, when she washed all the dishes. She knew the next day when the cycle of work repeated itself. The next week, her spirit saw the exit opportunity drift away, all while Doug David grew her children in her womb without having to try.

CHAPTER TWENTY

DD was heavy with the baby. Her mother told her that the birth would come soon. It's not that DD had *no* knowledge of how babies were born, not after all the lectures and sermons about it once she and Trout were found out. It was just that all the pregnancy and birthing and mothering information that DD got was filtered through her own mother and Rosie. And, to be honest, Carly had never sought medical help for any of her pregnancies, so she didn't have much more information than the few books she'd brought home many years ago.

DD did not distrust Rosie, exactly, but her track record as a mother was, at best, one win (Trout) and one loss (Pike). Plus Rosie's choice of mate did nothing to instill confidence in DD about how much help she'd get from her. Further, DD had noticed a distinct chill between her parents over the past month or two. And, true to form, when she asked about it, each parent had said some variation of *mind your own business* to her. Her mother resolutely refused to go to the glade with DD, which was a very bad sign. Her mother's surety and bravery had dissipated like smoke from a dead campfire. She often thought of the purity of the glade, the truth they could speak to each other there, and longed for that sanctuary.

One day when DD had walked—waddled—to the river, which led her past the cabins that Alaine had built, she saw him sitting on his steps. She grimaced a smile at him but kept going. She withered and her step faltered when he rose to his feet and angled towards her.

"DD, hello. I would speak with you if I may."

"I have a choice?"

He laughed. "Not really, no," he said when his chuckle ended. "I need to tell you a very important Truth."

"You do, huh?" she said wryly and stopped walking. "Why do I think this will be something I don't like?"

"Ah, youth," he mocked. "So often rebellious for no reason other than to seek originality."

"Let me be honest first, Alaine. I just don't like you. I don't trust you. And I wish my parents had asked my opinion—or I would have been old enough to be clear—when you first tromped mud on our porch when I was little."

She faced him on the dirt path, halfway between the cabins and the river where the cottonwood stood. She looked straight into his eyes with more resolve than she'd ever had when speaking with him. "You have been a cancer on my life and on my family. I wish you would leave."

He frowned at her. Took a deep breath. "Fine. You are now, even more than when you got with child, deserving of Judgment. The Lord has given me a Word," he pontificated. "Your defiance and disrespect and dishonor confirms that I must deliver this Word to you now. Today."

"I can't wait. Let me guess? I'm going to hell?" she smirked.

Though she spoke brave words, DD was not used to conflict. She'd been in a subservient role all her life. She had no other role models to show her what would be possible. Yet, with all that baggage, her motherhood insisted on showing itself at that moment. A baby to protect, even though she had no real idea what that meant, rose above all other allegiances. In that moment, her motherhood forged her into a fledgling warrior ready to battle in defense of the tiny child still onboard.

"You will never see your baby, DD," Alaine intoned.

He had the temerity to raise a hand at her, the reverse of a benediction. A *malediction* spoken at her from his twisted sense of his god.

"I will take that child from you," he continued preaching, "because you do not deserve to keep a child. Not when you are in a state of shame. A state of Shame, both from your wanton ways and from your misguided sense of importance. My Compound of

Kingdom Prophecy will prevail without you. Indeed it will flourish when your poison is removed."

When she spoke next, her voice quavered with fear and anger even while she stood firm, "What does that mean? In English, if you please. For those of us who are hell-bound?"

"It means!" he began with a shout. He took a breath, then spoke more calmly, "It *means* that all four of us adults agree that we will take your baby when it is born and remove it to somewhere else. Off the Compound. Where it will have a chance to live a life useful to others. You do not get to have—*keep*—a baby, is what that means!"

DD stood now with her hands in fists stacked on her hips. Her shoulders thrown back and her stomach round as a watermelon molded to her otherwise-thin frame. "You don't get to decide that! I choose. I am the mother. I will choose. Me!" she yelled. "And, furthermore," she continued in a brave voice, "your math is wrong. My mother will no longer tolerate your absurdity. Don't you dare count her among your votes."

He laughed at her, softly at first. Then threw his head back and cackled. Raised his hands to heaven with a look of disbelief on his face, as if God was actually listening to him. "You are not in charge, DD. If you think you will have any control over what slides out of your body at birthing time—if you think Pike or I will *let* you have any control—you are crazier than I am."

With that, he turned on his heel and strode away.

Shocked at his confession of insanity—hadn't he confessed he was crazy?—DD stood there wondering who would protect her baby when the time came.

CHAPTER TWENTY-ONE

"Alaine? I need to lay something at your feet," Mitchell said.

He stood at the doorway of the red cabin, Alaine's refuge from the world and his mountaintop to seek the Lord's face. Thus the red paint, scarlet like the burning bush. It didn't bother Alaine that the bush was, geographically, not in the same place Moses went to get the Commandments.

"Alaine?" he tried again.

"Mitchell. Come join me. I'm in prayer," he heard faintly from inside.

Mitchell heeled his boots off and stepped across the threshold in dingy socks, scuffing across the wood flooring.

"Kneel with me."

Mitchell did so, starting, "Alaine, I—"

"Hush. For a moment. Wait three cries of the jay, then speak your burden," Alaine commanded.

Even knowing this technique as a common one Alaine used, both to establish control of the pace of any given prayer meeting, and as a moment for the frantically beating heart to settle, Mitchell resented it. As the third bird began a song (not a jay, they both knew), he spoke. "My daughter is with child," he muttered. "She says it's Trout, but, of course, I don't trust her to be truthful."

Alaine had already had his confrontation with DD, so he knew well what Mitchell was coming to him for. He stifled a laugh, and said solemnly, "Ah. And so the cycle continues."

"What's that supposed to mean?" Mitchell asked, thrown off.

Alaine looked at him with a patronizing smile. "You do know, do you not, how we came to be here on this farm?"

"I know what you told me way back when. But I fail to see what that has to do with my daughter?" Mitchell objected, trying to regain his footing with Alaine. A small voice in the back of his head asked him to number the times Alaine had done this to him: threw him off his original purpose by changing the course. Diverting the water, as it were, of the creek. So only Alaine's crops and ideas got watered.

"Rosie is the mother of Pike and Trout," Alaine reminded him.

"Yes. And?" Mitchell said impatiently.

"I am not the father. I am merely their Guide."

"Still, I don't understand." Mitchell showed a truculence that he normally hid while Alaine spoke.

"Where do you think those two boys were conceived? Where is their father? Why isn't he the one raising them?" Alaine asked with increasing fervor.

"I don't know any of that! I can't even see why I should care! I want to know what to do about my daughter," Mitchell pleaded.

"You don't know any of that because *I removed them from that!* Just like I'm about to do with your daughter's spawn," he stated. "She stays here on the Compound until she births, then you may let her leave. We keep the baby and raise it as our own. But the thorn is what happens to you and Carly, not what happens to your child. And her child," Alaine added.

A declaration from a king that didn't care what the norm was, what the rule was.

Mitchell's attention had been arrested by several things Alaine said, but he decided to start at the first that bothered him. "Wait. You've done this before? You've taken children before?"

"Like I said, Rosie made a choice. Rosie had a choice. Which I see now was less than ideal. That's why, this time, we do it a different way."

Alaine saw little point in explaining the finer issues of where he found Rosie and what their agreement had been. He saw that Mitchell needed a redirect, and using Rosie and the boys as an ancient historical example of Alaine's power over people made sense to him.

"So... you took Rosie away from the birth father along with her babies?" Mitchell asked doubtfully.

Alaine opened his hands and said with a disarming smile, "She willingly came with me when I came upon her in a café. I could see she and her little tykes were hungry and didn't have money. It was as easy as feeding them, and they came with me."

"The father?"

"I never asked. Rosie never volunteered."

"So he could still be out there, looking for her and the boys?" Mitchell wondered.

"Why in the world would he? It's been years," Alaine said dismissively. "It was then that I felt the Call upon me. And that Call led me, after years of wandering the Wilderness, straight to your farmhouse door. The one you still walk through daily."

Alaine rarely referenced the five years it had taken them to get out to the Fox farm and ingratiate themselves onto the property. Their path of failed rental lives wasn't convenient to Alaine's narrative, and he was pretty sure Mitchell wouldn't think of those years, either. Not to question, anyway.

"Alaine, I thought it was all clear to me that we should follow the rules of the Compound. The rules that you set up, incidentally, to protect us all. But this? This doesn't sound right. It sounds like you are asking me and Carly to stay, keeping the baby, and banishing Doug David."

"Yes. That is my Will. Because it is the Lord's Will. My Will that young, irresponsible, not-quite-women should not benefit from their sin," Alaine admonished.

"What's to happen to Trout, then?"

Alaine waited a moment, then shook his head and said, "Why should anything happen to Trout?"

"He's the father," Mitchell said, his tone firm. "It's his sin, too, isn't it?"

Alaine gave a rueful and quiet chuckle. "Mitchell, you said yourself you don't trust Doug David to be truthful. Trout isn't necessarily the father. And it wouldn't be his fault, anyway. She's far too forward."

Mitchell shifted on his knees, then pushed himself to his feet. He realized that there was no other option for a father. Not when he'd heard how DD felt. He decided then and there to call Alaine on his bullshit. Whatever caul had fallen over his eyes since Alaine had come onto the porch those many years ago slipped away, and fury filled him. He turned to leave the cabin. "I do not accept your decision, Alaine!" he said over his shoulder. "I'll do with my family what I please!"

"Not true. Not even remotely," Alaine retorted, raising his voice. "Does the ship decide where the cyclone takes him?"

Mitchell stopped in the doorway and wheeled around. His shoulders drawn back, his rebooted feet spread apart nearly as far as the door's width. His fists clenched tightly enough for his skin to be drained of blood, and white against the blue of his jeans. "You are not a cyclone! You're just a man, and a lying, selfish one at that. You need to get your things, take those whom you wish, and leave my property." He turned on his heel and left. Mitchell's rage and brooding nature sent him to care for the livestock and mull what had changed, rather than return to the farmhouse right away and figure out a plan with Carly and DD.

Alaine rose slowly from his knees, which popped from sitting so long, shaking his head side to side, clucking his tongue. He put his own boots on and walked two cabins over to the one that Trout and Pike stayed in, clomping onto the small porch so they'd know it was him.

Later that night Doug David went into labor. After confronting Alaine, she'd drifted in and out of sleep. Had the phone line still been connected, Mitchell believed he would have already called for some help. Had Mitchell still had his car keys—when had Alaine taken *those,* he wondered—he'd have driven them off the farm and to a hospital. Carly was furious; she'd railed and wept and pleaded with him and done the same thing with Rosie. Now that the time was here, it was too late to do anything but hope Doug David, at least in body if not in conscious spirit, could deliver the baby. "Alive, if that's alright with you," Carly muttered at God.

Carly knew that Alaine was keeping track of the labor. He was making Rosie be there to help, and his thinly-veiled threats against Pike and Trout pinned her to the room. Alaine knew that would work; Rosie was always a weak-willed spirit if there was ever a threat to her precious boys. What filled Carly with wrath was knowing that Alaine not only held all the puppet strings but he also sat blithely uncaring while lives hung in the balance. She wanted to slap him. She wished mortal harm on him. Almost as much as she wanted to slap herself for letting it get to this point. She promised herself she'd have a long talk with Mitchell once they got free to figure out how they'd let it get this bad.

Alaine sat easily in the easy chair he'd found a while ago. He hooked a leg over one arm support. Waved a hand back and forth as he listened for noise from the *birthing house* as he liked to call it. "Lord, these people are stupid," he marveled.

This situation reminded him of that first town he lived in after he left his father. When he finally couldn't stand their idiot ways any longer and he told them off and moved on. He decided that if the next day didn't go his way—gaining control over the baby and regaining control over the narrative—it was time to cut his losses and shove off. Alone, if necessary. He would try to massage the unraveling situation for 12 more hours, but after that, he was done.

None of those personal dynamics pierced the haze surrounding Doug David when she was conscious. Between contractions, she slept. Or passed out. Carly couldn't tell. Mitchell sat in their kitchen wringing his hands. Rosie paced in the bedroom where Doug David and Carly were, but she could barely offer any coherent thought, let alone much assistance to the birth. The contractions woke Doug David, and it was at those times that her eyes would unglaze just long enough for her to bear down when her mama pleaded with her to push.

Long into the evening, a baby nudged out and slid into Carly's arms. As Carly held her granddaughter, wiping her eyes and mouth so she could breathe, Doug David pushed again. A second granddaughter that Carly caught one-handed started crying immediately. Because Rosie was in a stupor, and Mitchell had left the entire house after *not* hearing a cry from a baby,

Chapter Twenty-One

Carly was left to provide the immediate care for the tiny girls.

Rosie roused herself after a while. Helped Carly prop each baby at a breast of Doug David's, even though DD was still in a fog. Between Rosie and Carly and DD, they managed to get both babies to nurse for at least one session. It was enough to drop the twins into sleep, anyway. Rosie took them off their mama, wrapped each of them in a towel, and assured Carly that she'd lay them down right in the next bedroom.

"You've had a long day," Rosie said to Carly. "I'm sorry I was no help there; do you want to shut your eyes for just a second? I can wake you in fifteen minutes or a little longer. We can make sure Doug David is fine and all that in a bit. It won't hurt to rest."

Carly shook with exhaustion. The adrenaline of the day—of the last few days—had frazzled her system so hard that her eyelids fluttered. She stepped towards Rosie but her legs betrayed her. She dropped to a knee on the floor beside the bed where Doug David still lay. "We need to take care of her right now, don't you think?" Carly remembered only the birth of her two dead boys, which is to say, she didn't remember anything she did that worked, so it was mostly trauma that swirled around her thoughts.

"She'll be fine for a few minutes," Rosie said firmly. "The babies will sleep for a while, too. I've got them set up. I'll come get you in a few; trust me."

"Fifteen minutes, no more," Carly said, lifting one finger at Rosie, even as she headed to a bedroom to sleep.

Rosie interacted with DD and Carly with a straight, open, trusting face. She could tell that it had all gone sour on the Fox farm. She recognized Alaine's warning signs, and knew that he was about to cut his losses and leave. Her spirit battled between getting these two brand-new babies to safety or getting her own boys out from under Alaine's thumb. Whatever she needed to do for that to happen is what she would do.

Rosie waited. Watched both mother and daughter, defenseless now, while they recovered. She hoped they'd both live, she really did, but it was beyond her control. It really was. She decided to take the babies before Alaine could; who knew what evil ritual he was dreaming up right this second to get his place back at the top.

Sitting in his cabin, Alaine heard the slam of the farmhouse door when Mitchell left, saw him stride off towards the water. He heard one baby cry—he was too far away to hear the grizzling of the second one, so didn't know it was two—and decided that he could work on his speech to claim the baby for the Kingdom Prophecy Compound.

Mitchell walked slowly back to the main house and in the back door. When he didn't find his wife in the kitchen, he climbed the steps to the bedroom they still shared. She lay on the bed, curled into a ball, her back to the door. The blinds were closed and the curtains were closed, too. It was dark in there.

"Carly?"

She rolled so she was on her back. Turned her head towards him.

"We've done a terrible thing, Mitchell."

Mitchell's face darkened like storm clouds off in the distance. "I hate to say it, but you're right, Carly. We're in a jam," he admitted. "I'm pretty sure it's my fault for letting him talk to me on the porch."

She sat up on the bed and pushed herself upright against the headboard. "I never should have let you let that man in the house, Mitchell," she spat. "He has been the ruin of our lives. You know it and I know it. It was only ever gonna end this way, and I'm furious that I let it go the way he wanted!"

"Did you try to tell me, though?" Mitchell objected. "I didn't see it until now."

Carly slumped back, shaking her fists, crying in frustration. She climbed from the bed, keeping it between them. She realized, or maybe admitted to herself, that Mitchell wasn't smart enough to see it. And, just like a physics professor doesn't chide a grade schooler learning division, she decided not to take her anger out on Mitchell. They'd have to figure it out from here onward. Blame could come later.

"Mitchell. Baby. We had a good thing! It is long gone, but remember? When we started? We had it all. All of it," she groaned. "And it's all turned to shit now. We've got to go get DD and we've got to go get those babies and we have to leave. Right now!"

"The babies haven't gone anywhere, Carly. They're still here. Rosie has them downstairs. And I agree. Get a bag packed and let's go."

They both, finally, shared a clarity of purpose just then and started to see a way through. Carly put a hand on Mitchell's chest, grateful, and went to get their things.

CHAPTER TWENTY-TWO

Rosie lunged forward from the rocker in the nursery and leapt to her feet. Two little babies slept and a wave of peaceful love swept over her. This sensation, so rare for her to feel, was what she imagined when Alaine presented his vision to her of a "place along a river, where God's faithful could gather and flourish." She'd made the decision to remove the twin babies before anything bad could happen to them.

On her way to the car, Mitchell's keys in hand, Alaine intercepted her. He spoke to her before she could leave. "The only way that baby lives is if you take it far away and raise it as your own. Or give it to someone who will keep their mouth shut about where it came from."

"They're twins," Rosie said. "That's what I'm doing. And you're insane."

"Twins, huh? I hadn't heard. That's a sign of favor, for sure," Alaine exulted.

"How can it be a sign of favor? You've already banished them from your precious Compound!" Rosie scoffed. "You'll never escape this, Alaine. I should have left you a long time ago! The last thing I'll say to you is let my boys go free before it all goes to shit."

"Still," he tilted his head as he conceded. "The Lord can do great things with twins, even if it is somewhere away from here. And your boys are in it to the end now. They've both got a role to play."

"DD wants to keep them. I'm sure of it. Her parents do, too," Rosie said, not bothering to rebut any of his last comments.

Alaine equally ignored her remark and asked, "Have you seen Mitchell and Carly speak to each other at all? I haven't. At least not in the last two months. They are in no position to—"

"Spare me. You've done nothing but drive spikes between us all. I see it now and wish I'd seen it sooner," Rosie declared.

Her voice dripped with both sarcasm and fatigue. Rosie was sick and tired of how long Alaine had run his game on her, on her boys, and now on Mitchell, Carly, and DD. She hated herself for not leaving years ago, whether Trout and Pike would have come along or not. But now that yet another generation was going to be ruined by his megalomaniacal delusions, the elastic snapped. "I'm leaving with them and won't be coming back," she told him.

He smiled at her. "That's the best outcome I could hope for, Rosie. You take care now."

She recognized that look on his smug face and wanted to punch it. She vowed she'd never end up in a place where this kind of person was, and yet... maybe she'd never left. After Doyle's dysfunctions had chased them out of their basement apartment and she got on a bus that went for days and, finally, when she was out of money and Alaine offered to buy them all food, she was grateful for the rescue. Well, that was survival, wasn't it? And she couldn't bear to think that she'd traded one bad penny for another. Until now, when there was no other option but to face the ugly truth.

"I'll let you think you've won, Alaine. I'll take the babies and I'll find them a home. But I'm not coming back," she repeated.

Alaine countered her resolve with a threat, and an offer. "You come back, and your boys can leave. If you don't come back, they will have outlived their usefulness. If you catch my meaning." Gloating. Speaking as if he'd already won.

"I've always caught your meaning. You're not that inscrutable. You're an ass. I'll let you say my goodbyes to my boys and let the wind do with us all what it will."

"That's a mighty casual way to dismiss the Will of the Lord, Rosie," he said derisively. "I imagine you'll be quite surprised when you see Judgment come down upon you."

"If his judgment," she flicked her fingers in air quotes, "means I never have to listen to your puling drivel again, then I count myself a winner. Good riddance."

Alaine frowned as he walked back to the cabin, thinking that had not gone as he wished. But since she agreed to remove the baby—babies!—he filed it away as "good enough" and moved on to plot against his next quarry.

Pike and Trout had known that DD was in labor. They'd seen enough livestock drop babies that they understood the general timeline of what was to follow. What Pike didn't know was if Alaine would really send the baby away. And if Trout would let that happen, let alone would DD's parents let that happen. Pike hadn't seen Trout around much in the last few days; surprising since 40 acres with a mix of crops and livestock, a handful of buildings, two cars, and an old canoe were the only things that could occupy a person.

"I don't give a shit what Trout is up to, anyway," Pike muttered to himself. "That idiot can go suck on it."

Pike wandered away from the cedars behind his cabin and out to the front of Alaine's. He'd see what needed doing. About that same time, Alaine moved quickly across the yard from the river and stopped right in front of Pike. Alaine looked upset.

"Pike! I'm glad I found you," he huffed.

"Hey, there. It's been boring around here—what's going on?" Pike asked idly.

"Well, you know about DD beginning the birthing? Right?"

"Yup. We heard enough a while ago when she started to grunt and holler and stuff, so I came back here to get out of earshot. Cows and pigs don't make that kind of ra—"

"Shut up for a second, Pike. We have a real problem."

Pike tried so hard not to show his hurt feelings that he couldn't finish his sentence about how quiet animals are when they give birth. He'd wanted to tell Alaine that it was because animals still had an instinct about predators. He settled for repeating his first statement.

"Fine. Like I said. What's goin' on?"

Alaine scuffed the dirt, looked down at it, looked back up at Pike. Nodded his head once. "I'm gonna have to trust you, Pike."

"Why wouldn't you ever?" Pike marveled.

"I *do.* That's why I've gotta tell you. Mitchell and Carly are gonna make a run for the law," Alaine finished in a low voice tinged with defeat.

This was a thing that Alaine had drilled into Pike and Trout since they were first introduced to him, way back when they were little. *Do not trust a policeman or any kind of law man!* Alaine had spun every story of when he was on the run so that the *long arm of the law* was corrupt and rotten and always out to get the independent thinkers. That *going to the law* was the worst possible outcome and almost certainly meant that the person doing it was corrupt themselves and trying to take Alaine down with them.

"Why in the world would they do that?" Pike said in disbelief. "I thought they called you leader?"

"Oh, it's worse! It's way worse than what it looks like! They told me they're going to the law because they think that Trout, and maybe *you* raped DD and got her pregnant! And since she isn't 18, we are all gonna be guilty of it. And... I hate to say this, Pike, but DD does not like you. Not one bit."

"What the heck did I do to get included here?" he snarled. "I ain't never been with her and that's the truth."

Alaine's eyes shifted as he saw Pike take the bait of outrage. "Pike, listen, I *get* it. You're gonna be the first one in handcuffs and the last one—maybe the only one—who deserves better! I'm just not sure what I can do to stop them from leaving."

Alaine laid that last line down gently. Like floating a hooked worm on a bobber slowly past a huge catfish so the fish wouldn't startle. Alaine waited to see if Pike could do the math and come to the right conclusion. The only conclusion.

Pike pulled his lips in and pushed them out, scratched his scraggly bearded chin, took his folding knife out of his pocket and fiddled with the blades. He looked up at Alaine, who stood almost a head taller than him. "You think we oughta stop 'em?"

Alaine had started doing a combination nod and shake of his head before Pike was finished asking the question. "Do you see any other way?"

"I sure don't." Although Pike regularly told anyone who would listen that he was *not an idiot*, he had a lot of blind spots. Pike would never win in a battle of wits or intelligence, but he had a cunning in him that was deeper, older than intelligence. A survival cunning that assessed risk and provided solutions without the burden of morality. "I can stop them, Pa," he said. "I'll just take my rifle and wait for them by the cars. If they don't quit when I ask 'em to, I'll put 'em down."

"Ah, God, Pike. Are you sure?"

"Like I said, it's us or them."

He'd said no such thing, but Alaine would not dream of stopping the motion that Pike had started. Alaine forced sadness into his face to override his glee and put his hand on Pike's shoulder. "You've got to, I guess. I thank you. You're one of the good ones. Godspeed."

Pike turned on his heel towards his cabin, opened the door, reached around to snag the rifle, and headed for the fence line and the road. He glanced over his shoulder at Alaine, waggled the rifle, and walked out of sight.

❖

After Mitchell and Carly had decided to leave, he went into the bedroom where Doug David lay in the bed. He double-checked to see if she had the babies sleeping with her. It was just DD there.

He heard Carly say from the hallway, "Rosie's not out there, but I'll check the downstairs like you said."

"Did she say she'd keep the babies?" Mitchell asked.

"Yeah, Rosie got them asleep and was going to wake me in a few minutes. What time is it?"

"It's long past dark. I've been outside for hours. I'm sorry; it was just too much like the boys for me."

"Same here. I thought I could push through, but I needed to shut down for a second," she said. "Wait a minute? You said you were out there for hours?"

"Oh, yeah. At least two," he said grimly.

"We should have heard them wake up by now. Go see if the babies are asleep next room! Right now," Carly ordered with alarm.

Mitchell left the room and clumped down the steps.

"Not down here, Carly!" he yelled up the stairway. "I'll check the front porch!"

Carly took a last look at DD, sleeping peacefully it seemed, and tore down the stairs to join Mitchell outside.

"Nowhere!" Mitchell exclaimed. "I can't find Rosie out here, either!"

Rosie had left the farm in the one sedan that was still running, at least an hour before Mitchell and Carly realized anything was amiss. Alaine had heard her go, but the boys didn't know that she left. She only made a mile or two down the road before she parked the car, on a farmer's wheat field drive, and had her own bout of shaking, fueled by adrenaline.

"I can't save my boys if I'm not there. This isn't right no matter what," Rosie lamented with her head on the steering wheel.

As far as she could tell, in her foggy state, her fight-or-flight response had insisted she leave. Now, away from Alaine and the messy, bloody birth room, it didn't make any sense at all. She knew she'd need to go back. To give the babies back. And take her older ones with her instead. But she remained paralyzed by indecision.

"Mama?" DD called out. "Mother?" She got increasingly frantic. "Is anyone there?" The last clear thought she had was Alaine's speech to her about not having any control over her baby. Babies, she at least knew that much now. Rosie and Carly had been there to help. Had cleaned and wrapped the babies in soft felt blankets. In response to DD's repeated inquiries about her father, Rosie only had said, "He can't be in here right now." Rosie gave no explanation as to why, and DD was too exhausted to stick with the thought.

Now, upon waking in the upstairs bedroom, DD was alone. She could tell. She wouldn't stay that way for long. Not when her babies were missing, her parents were missing, her entire reason for being in question.

Once Pike had walked off to do sentry duty, Alaine went in search of Trout. As much as he needed Pike to be the assassin, he needed Trout to trust Alaine for one more day. He found Trout out back of the cabin, in a hammock strung between the old clothesline posts. "Trout, I'm glad I found you. Trout?"

Trout opened his eyes and looked around, owly from sleep.

"How can you sleep at a time like this?" Alaine said derisively. "You've always been quick to escape."

"I—it's hard. The waiting, I mean. I've been waiting for news of the baby and DD. You know I haven't slept in the last day or two. It just caught up with me," Trout yawned. He had awoken slowly, but the derision and accusation from Alaine rapidly pulled him into a sickly awareness.

Alaine stood over him and wagged his head side to side as he said, "Ah. Yes. Well. Not everyone has the discipline to be alert for the Tricks of the Enemy."

"Tricks? What tricks?" Trout struggled to get out of the hammock; he flicked a leg out which almost overturned the whole thing. He gracelessly flopped out of the hammock onto one knee, flailing one arm up and one arm to the ground to stop his motion. He brushed the dirt off his pants as he stood.

Alaine didn't put a hand out to help. He sneered a chuckle at Trout, making sure he saw disdain on his face mixed with a little pity.

"What tricks are you talking about, Alaine?" Trout repeated.

"This whole thing! It's a mess. It's not legal, it's not lawful, it's surely going to result in trouble for you," Alaine said in a confiding voice.

"Trouble for me? What did I do?" Trout said plaintively.

Alaine smirked again. "You mean other than having sex—possibly against her will—with a legally-defined child? You mean forbidding her to seek medical attention? You mean separating her from her parents? That kind of trouble?"

"I didn't do any of that!"

"No?" Alaine shook his head, running his rueful mask again—he'd gotten a lot of use out of it lately—and clucking his tongue. "Well, who's to say? All I know is what I heard from Mitchell and Carly and DD talking in there. Between contractions, I mean. They say it's your fault."

Alaine acted like he was sorry it was happening this way, but a smile played at the corners of his mouth. Trout opened his mouth to protest, but Alaine held his hands up. "I know! You've done nothing wrong! I tried to tell them that, but they weren't in a mood to listen."

"I've got to go see her! I don't want bad blood between us!" Trout cried.

Alaine soothed, "Listen, Trout, that's just not a good idea. Right now. I mean, it is a good idea, but just not now. They need to get that baby out and then get rested and then get to thinking straight again. And, of course, only in my humble opinion, you need to stay out of their sight until all that can happen."

"I can't just sit here, can I ?" Trout said worriedly.

"I think you gotta. You can't rush nature," Alaine chuckled.

"This isn't a joke, Alaine!" Trout yelled. "I love her. I'm gonna love that baby!"

"Of course. Of course! I don't mean to make it a joke; you've just got to be patient. Twenty-four hours, maybe a few more. Maybe even in the morning, in the light of day. Let me go work the problem. You stay out of it. I'll get to DD first, after the baby is born, and go from there. I think she likes you, too," Alaine conceded.

Alaine knew well and good that there were two babies. But he wasn't about to tell Trout. Not when Trout was off balance and fuzzy from sleep and could barely stand still for want of rushing to try and fix the problem which would make it way worse. No, Alaine needed Trout to stay out of the picture until Rosie was clear of the property and Pike had dealt with DD's parents. With Trout back on the chessboard, there were simply too many variations to count on winning. He'd come back in a few hours, long enough for Trout to drop off again, to tell him the next phase of his spin.

❖

"Trout, she doesn't want them," Alaine said hours later, exactly as he had planned.

Trout hadn't slept, but he obeyed Alaine by staying at their end of the Compound, stirring coals and sticks of firewood into a smoky fire. When Trout heard that come out of Alaine's mouth, he slumped to the ground. He'd just stood back up from more exhausted sleep. But a wash of dizziness, nausea, and a looseness in his bowels dropped him right back down to the ground. "I can't think straight. I think I'm sick with something," Trout mumbled. "Tell me again what she said?"

Alaine clucked his tongue, shook his head, waved his hands down low near his waist.

"Tell me!" Trout demanded.

"Ah, Trout," Alaine said with mock regret. "You're already a knocked-down horse. I hate to kick you."

"Tell me!" shouted Trout.

If Trout had been thinking clearly, if he had been free from the sickness—whatever it was—flushing him, if he had lived a normal life where a person his age studied malignant personalities in school, he would have seen right through Alaine's act. As it was, he believed that Alaine was delivering accurate and devastating news to him. Trout had finally seen that he wanted a different life than what he had. He wanted a life with DD. And he wanted to see that baby.

"She said it plain as day," Alaine recounted, as if it were true. "I've rarely heard her be so clear and decisive; you know how women are. She told me to tell you." He paused, took a breath. "Told me to send you away. Send you away with these words: 'Tell him he's caused enough trouble in my life and I don't want him around anymore.' "

"She didn't. She loves me. I love her," Trout moaned.

"I'm sorry, son. She did."

"Why should I believe you?" Trout asked, a faint existential dread wanting first-hand testimony rather than hearsay.

Alaine plowed past his objection; a bulldozer smoothing out a washboarded country road. "Why should you believe me? Why should you believe *me*— the Lord's own Servant? I've spoken only Truth even when many—*many*—have spoken ill of me! I would find a different way to share these truths with you. But there is no hiding from the noonday pitiless sun of her words. I'm sorry, Trout. She's done with you."

Trout stayed slumped on the ground, tears making tracks down his unwashed face. Alaine stood long enough to see if any spirit would return in the boy. When he saw that Trout was a completely whipped dog, utterly defeated and without options, Alaine walked away, whistling.

Trout woke up filled with rage. He jumped to his feet and stomped to Alaine's cabin.

"Your mild and holy act doesn't work anymore! You can open this door and open it *now*," Trout yelled from the muddy porch.

Pike had tried to rush him when he stepped onto the porch and, as a consequence, was laid out flat on the floor after Trout used the butt of his rifle on Pike's face. Pike groaned and moved his legs heavily on the floor.

"I'll put you *down*, Alaine," Trout barked. "I've had it! You tell me the truth and no *bullshit* or I'll shoot you through and through," he vowed through gritted teeth.

"Come in, son," Alaine said when Trout finally swung the door open wide. "Of course I have no idea what you are discomposed about."

Alaine sat in his prayer warrior chair: an old rocker with sweat-stained cushions, with a greasy blanket across his lap. This was all inside Alaine's cabin that neither son—stepson—was allowed into without an express physical and verbal invitation from only Alaine.

"You are the main problem on this entire property, and I've been too blind to see it," Trout shouted. "Too deeply in debt to you to get it. It's finally over, though, and I don't owe you anything anymore!"

Pike sat up and slid himself over to the wall to prop himself up.

Trout pointed at him in fury. "And you don't owe him anything, either, Pike! For once in your life listen to me. Realize that he's a puppet master; all he does is pull your strings, my strings, all of our strings to keep him king for one more day."

"Oh, I think Pike owes me a thing or two, still," Alaine smirked. "Or did I not hear a few gunshots a while ago?"

Pike paled, even more than he already was from Trout's beating.

"What did you do, Pike?" Trout begged. "What did he make you do?"

"Yes, Pike. Please. Tell us." Alaine added in a low, menacing tone, like when he started a new section of sermon that would build to a condemnation, "What did you do all on your own accord?"

❖

Earlier that last night, Pike had stood watch over the driveway, with his rifle and both his lizard survival instinct plus his need for Alaine's approval. He could see the sedan. He could see the road. He couldn't quite see the gate, but there was no way to get to the gate unless a person... who was he fooling? Unless Mitchell and Carly walked through his field of view.

For all the times Pike got sleepy while hunting or fishing, for all the times his mind wandered, it was a possibility that Mitchell and Carly could slip by without alerting him. In a just world, that is exactly how it would happen. Mitchell and Carly, recent revelations awakening them into tandem trust, would get away, find someone in authority who could stop this awful train, and get DD reunited with those two perfect, living, breathing babies. Like they couldn't do before.

Pike, though, was laser focused and saw them. Didn't need the scope: they were plain as day in the cast from the barnyard light. The only grace those two received was that Pike didn't think it was necessary to kill them. He had decided that they just needed to be constricted to the property, and after it settled down, Alaine could decide their final fates.

He shot them both, once each, through the leg right near the hip. It was an easy shot with the rifle.

He took his time. He used the scope to study each face after each shot. Enjoyed the pain and panic flashing across them. They fell to the ground, almost like synchronized dancers at the end of a routine. He watched them for a while, waiting to see if they would be able to move towards the car and freedom. No. The arc of justice sloped downward still for those two; no way for them to see if it would ever turn in their favor.

Trout had been the one to shoot Alaine. There was no other way, not once Trout asked him to turn himself and Pike in, and Alaine started in on the "I'm the great deliverance and prophet of the Lord" speech. Trout knew, far too well, how long it would take to get him wound back down, hell, even to get a word in edgewise, when he got himself into that state.

"Daddy, you'd better shut up now," Pike said, faithful to the last in calling him Daddy.

"I'll thank you to show some respect to your elders, and to Listen to the Word of God," Alaine had started with outrage.

"Last warning, Alaine, or I'll put you down," Trout breathed.

As Alaine drew another deep, indignant breath to begin a fresh round of berating, Trout casually lifted the rifle to his waist, barely aiming, and put one round through him. Alaine fell onto the braided rug in the front room, gasping at the pain.

"That's my answer, Alaine. I'm leaving now. And may God have mercy on our souls for what we've done here," Trout said, his voice full of sadness.

CHAPTER TWENTY-THREE

When Rosie left, she made do with what she had on hand, and that was a nest for the babies in the footwell of the old sedan with dubious license plates. She had thrown a few things in a bag before scooping the babes up and heading for the car.

She turned left out of the property. "The Compound, my ass," she scoffed, and then turned south at the first paved road she came to. After her brief pullover where she decided who to save, she traveled on. It's not like she hadn't driven at all since they got there, but she was for sure rusty. She took it slow. Rarely drove over 50 mph, and slowed nice and early for all the intersections she came to. Rural drivers in that part of the state of Kansas fit two broad categories: big trucks with nothing flashy and usually hauling something—a trailer or an attachment for a bigger farm implement; and sedans with older people driving them. Rosie hated to think of herself as older, but that's what most of the people out driving saw her as. Another old lady driving back roads for some errand or another. Going nowhere fast.

She'd driven south for at least an hour. Long enough to cross into Oklahoma, though the sign on this road was pretty small and shared a post with the county sign. The babies had started fussing almost as soon as she hit Oklahoma, and Rosie stopped at an old Phillips 66 gas station with an attached convenience store that was less than five miles into the state. She cracked a window but left the babies in the footwell. She stretched a towel from the dashboard to the headrest, telling herself it was for sun protection, but knowing deep down that she didn't want any questions about her passengers.

Rosie gassed up, bought a small amount of baby formula, a travel pack of diapers (way too big), some wet wipes, plus a Coke and a hot dog for herself. She'd thrown in some powdered nutrition additive that they used for the calves if the mother wouldn't nurse them like she was supposed to. She had no idea if that would sustain the babies, but figured she'd dribble a little into their mouths and then see how they took it.

"I'm not keeping them very long, anyway," Rosie muttered, strapping back into the sedan.

"Let's go find you a home, girls," she crooned down at the babies. She drove away from the station to the first farm road out of town, where she parked, mixed some powder into the milk, and fed them both a few spoonfuls. Their mouths worked like they wanted to nurse. Rosie's own heart kind of cracked at that; realizing what she'd already robbed from them, which was a chance to nurse and sleep and feel safe with their real mama. "Too late now, girls. There was no other way."

They both grizzled and gummed the spoon with the mixture. It calmed them enough so she could change their diapers into the cavernous ones she'd just bought. She wrapped them tightly, like burritos, and they settled enough so she could put them back down and drive some more.

She found her way to Enid, Oklahoma. It wasn't a city by any stretch of the imagination, but it had more than its share of churches, which is what Rosie decided she was looking for. Surely one of these churches would have a food pantry, or a childcare ministry, or a clothing bank that she could walk into. She'd just have to talk her way past any of the objections they gave her and find a way to leave these two babies with a person who could keep their mouth shut.

Rosie had settled on a story that hinted at a domestic violence situation with a man who had connections to law enforcement in both states. She would sketch a story of her, as the well-meaning neighbor, trying to keep the babies safe until the mother had a chance to escape the dangerous living situation: *could be a week, could be months, who could know?* she'd say. Rosie would give the receiver a "recovery phrase" that, she would say, the mother and Rosie had agreed upon. So if and when the time came, the birth mother could take over again. She would impress upon them how important it was to keep any and all authorities out of it; the man had a strange hold over those who would decide who eventually got to keep the babies.

As she drove the grid of Enid's streets, secretly hoping for one last prompting from the Lord (even though she knew Alaine was ruined, she still believed in a Higher Being), she reviewed how she had gotten here. There was no other way to keep the babies alive—more than alive; unharmed—than to remove them immediately. She wished now that she had waited to talk to DD, for sure, and probably Mitchell and Carly. Sad, tragic, blood of her own womb, a danger to everything pure and good, she again affirmed that she'd made the right choice to let her boys sink or swim on their own.

Rosie turned a corner, saw a line of cars parked at a very old church. A few people standing just outside of a side door. One of the women had a scarf tied around her hair and she was holding a cake—maybe a pie?—in a plastic container. Rosie stopped the car, let it idle, put it in park. She rolled the window down and waved her hand at the woman with the plastic container.

The woman smiled at her. Took a few steps into the street. "Hi, there, hon, can I help you?" the woman asked.

"Hello," Rosie said.

"Are you looking for the Caring Mothers group meeting?" the woman asked with a smile.

"I think I am. Yes."

"You found it. We're right down the stairs after you get inside. It's not a big group, but we'd love to have you come visit," the woman encouraged.

"I think I'd like that. I have a problem. I'm hoping you all can help," Rosie admitted.

"Well, you come on in and we will get you what you need, hon."

Rosie waited until the cake woman walked back to the church and inside before she got out the driver's door and went to the passenger door. She took the two babies along with the small, almost pathetic bag of the few things she'd brought along. Deep breath, and then she entered the church.

The sign on the classroom door said *Caring Mothers Group* and a second, smaller line *in grief and joy, we support each other.* When Rosie went in, there were ten or 15 people, all women, sitting or standing as if they were waiting for someone to call them to attention. There were no other children there. By now, the two babies had woken and begun to fuss. It was quickly clear to Rosie who of the women had lost babies and who of them still had children at home, because of the crying. Women crying, that is, not the babies.

"Hello, there, hon. I'm glad you came in!" said the cake lady.

"Can we help you with those two angels?" said another voice.

"Oh, my gosh, I'd love to hold them!" exclaimed a third. "Anyone else miss these baby days?"

Rosie realized she was exhausted. Tears sprang to her eyes; she had no idea why. Her right leg twitched when she tried to take a step forward. To the group, maybe, it looked like she was falling. That was all it took for two women to take one baby each, another to rummage through the bag for food, or a pacifier, or a diaper. Someone led her to a loveseat that sat along the edge of the room, outside the circle of chairs that had been set up, and opposite the table of refreshments.

In due course, everyone had recovered enough so they felt comfortable asking Rosie to "tell us how we can help" her situation. Rosie, still woozy and fuzzy, presented the tale of the domestic abuse "in a nearby community" where the mother had asked her to "get her babies to safety and don't call the police," with enough authenticity to convince the women. At least, they acted like they understood the assignment and the importance of confidentiality. Although there were several offers to care for the babies, the winner was one of the sad ones; she said her home was already set up for children and she'd been considering a daycare, anyway, so it was really very little trouble and it would, indeed, be a blessing, maybe even a lifesaving one.

Rosie dutifully gave the new caregiver a phone number (only a few digits off of the real one at the Compound—and who knew if that phone still worked anyway?) to call if the burden ever got to be too much. Rosie took down several phone numbers and promised to call "as soon as the threat of violence has subsided" and assured them it would only be days or maybe a week before "someone reaches out to get the babies back to their mother."

After eating one too many pieces of cake (mystery of the container solved), Rosie excused herself, thanked them profusely and frenetically, got back in her car, and drove away. Once out of town, still a bit dazed, she crumpled the paper with the phone numbers on it and threw it out the window and into the slipstream while she drove west.

Rosie had no one now. She spent a few nights in one of those old-fashioned motor hotels on the outskirts of some town. A name she didn't remember. She slept. Showered. Even bought some clothes at a thrift store. She'd heard of a casino over near the interstate in Arizona that always needed workers, so she headed that way. She gave them the thinnest of resumes, offered to do anything but sex work, and assured them she didn't use any drugs. They hired her for kitchen help at first, saying they'd keep her in mind if there was something more glamorous that came along.

"I don't need glamorous," she told them. "Back in the kitchen is fine with me."

"Ok, Pansy, let's see how that goes for you. Welcome to the team," said the suit, with a handshake.

Pansy, as Rosie decided to call herself, drove past the main office to the employee dorm and toted her used, mostly empty suitcase into a room. Her heart remained a crusted and cracked shell. She thought, increasingly, about how happy she'd been with her two tiny little kids gamboling around her, always hungry, always laughing or crying, tugging on her. First her breasts for food as babies, then her hands for walking help, then her ankles when she moved away from their tantrums. Then she thought about how, by taking Doug David's twins away, she'd denied all those experiences to a young mother.

She picked up the phone. Put it back down. Wondered who, exactly, to call.

Housekeeping had an opening for a cleaner, which she took. She was fine until she started cleaning a room with playpens, diaper bags, and baby food in them. There was a day, near the end of her list of "to be cleaned," that she knocked, knocked again, used her master key to enter a room. It was mostly neat and would be an easy ten-minute job. In the corner, though, sat a playpen. Not unusual except there lay a small baby in it, sniffling quietly to himself. When the baby saw Rosie (with the Pansy name tag, which he couldn't read), he stood to his feet, stretched his arms out, and started screaming to be held.

Rosie stopped in the doorway. Looked at both the queen beds. No one in either. Stepped to the bathroom to see if someone was in there. No one there. She swept the shower curtain back to make sure. Also checked the small closet where the miniature ironing board hung.

The baby squalled. Snot ran down his nose. His eyes were red, swollen, full of pain. His diaper was bulging with pee. A pile of several old diapers sat next to the trash can, so the room smelled like piss and shit, anyway. She turned the ventilation fan on high, crossed to the playpen, and picked up the baby. He screamed right in her ear while she patted his back to try to get him down off the cliff of hysteria he'd parked himself on. Finally, she laid him down on the floor to change his diaper. Unpleasant, to say the least. She put fresh pants and shirt on him, too, and dug a plastic-covered baby spoon out of the bag, opening a jar of something orange and pureed.

He ate like he was starving. One jar down in no time at all. She got a cup of water from her cart, let him drink tap water from it. Although it seemed like a new experience for him, he got most of the water in his tummy, and very little of it on his fresh shirt, which had two kittens on it and *Hang in there, Baby!* Rosie sat holding him until his eyes drooped. She laid him back down in the play pen, cleaned the room quickly, exited and made sure the door was locked.

Rosie pushed her cart back to housekeeping central, stowed it in her bay, put her clipboard back on the hook after turning in her list of "rooms cleaned today." She sat on the sprung couch in one corner of the space, a small TV with rabbit ears showing a mid-day soap opera. She wasn't sure if she should tell someone about the baby or not. She didn't know if she would get in trouble for feeding the baby, changing the baby, putting him back down. All she knew was that time with a baby cracked all the scar tissue she'd built up over her heart and spirit all over again. She wept, wishing she could go back to get Doug David's babies, find Doug David, and help her raise those babies as any good grandmother would.

In the end, she settled for driving back to Enid, to that same old church, going inside to find a pastor there who listened to her story. The man promised her he'd find out what he could. No, she didn't want to leave a number. *Just find those babies is enough for me,* she'd told him. The least a grandmother could do.

The thing about state governments is that they *work*, they just work exceedingly *slowly*. The state of Kansas had reached a dead end in the search for the two babies that Doug David insisted were hers. That changed when a preacher called Kerri.

Part 5

MAC'S FARM, AGAIN

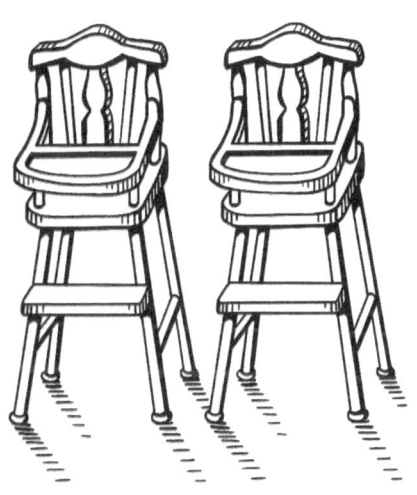

CHAPTER TWENTY-FOUR

It took almost a month before Mac convinced DD that they should call someone in the government to help them figure out what happened on the Fox farm. Once DD agreed and Mac called his long-time sheriff friend, they found out that no one was living out at DD's only home. The sheriff had found Alaine, dead by gunshot wound, and the bodies of Mitchell and Carly hugging each other in death. That had sparked news coverage, of course, but the sheriff had no knowledge of Rosie, Trout, Pike, or the babies. No weapons had been recovered, either.

Mac relayed the story of the babies, several times, to different people; sometimes over the phone, sometimes in person if they drove out to Mac's farm. The authorities were apologetic to DD about not having information regarding her babies, but, at the same time, didn't have any good answers. She finally made contact with a child welfare office who said they'd have someone contact her as soon as possible.

Doug David's case officer, an angel named Kerri, had spoken to her, faithfully, every month or so. Kerri had taken a personal interest in the case, more so than is usual for people already dedicated to saving as many as they can from the cruelty of others. Kerri had worked the welfare office and social issues job descriptions for years and years. She'd gotten so she had most of her counterparts in other states on her rolodex. They sent each other Christmas and birthday cards, and they tried to meet for a cookout once every summer, just to tell stories and bolster each other with encouragement.

Kerri didn't have to beg her boss for the extra time it would take to run down any and every rumor about the case. Her boss knew her well enough to not be surprised when Kerri walked in with the file in her hand.

"Let me guess," Loretta laughed. "You've got a hunch? And you want some extra time to pursue it?"

Kerri replied, "I just think if I could spend an hour a day, calling around, I could get at least *something.*"

"You're right; it's not ridiculous to think someone knows something," Loretta agreed. "Ok, you can use four hours of overtime a week. That's it. Talk to me in a month and we will see."

Of course, one month didn't produce any results. Kerri had gone back to her boss 13 times to ask for extra time, once each month. Loretta had reduced the overtime authorization to one hour a week, then finally telling Kerri there was just no way to justify it. At that, Kerri had acquiesced with no argument, which Loretta knew meant Kerri would be working on her own time over lunch and after hours. Kerri made all the calls from her office, respecting the ethics of the job, knowing that it would matter to a custody hearing that nothing untoward, at least on her end, had taken place.

She called her counterparts in a regular rotation; a pattern that was soothing to her. She would dutifully call Mac's phone to speak with DD, even if it was no news.

"We don't have any new information, I'm sorry to say," was her standard line.

"Have you stopped looking?" was Doug David's.

"I promise you that I have not. I'm looking."

They'd wish each other well, thank each other, and hang up the phone for another month. Kerri worked a lot of cases. Overworked like a typical state employee. An empath like many who end up working for social services. Kerri's heart broke each time she heard a new story of injustice or damage or abuse to children, and her resolve hardened with each story, too. She never took "no" for an answer the first time she interacted, and she had a reputation with the surrounding state offices. *A champion*, they'd say. *The gold standard*, they'd repeat to each other. Families seeking justice breathed easier once they got to know Kerri, knowing that if anyone could find a solution, it would be her.

It took a call from a puzzled clerk in Oklahoma for the case to advance. Kerri had already packed her now-empty lunch bag and her briefcase, ready to walk out the door. When she heard her friend Estelle's voice, from the Enid office, she set her things back down next to her desk and got a pad of paper out. Estelle relayed a conversation she had with a minister who'd had a visit from a woman who spoke of guilt about some babies dropped off over a year ago.

At last, a possible break. "Doug David, it's Kerri."

"Let me guess, no news?" she responded, tired from the day.

Kerri took a second before she answered. "Actually, I've had a call. From a church down in Enid, Oklahoma, about some babies that had been dropped off down there, over a year ago."

"They had babies dropped off?"

Kerri heard the hope rising in DD's voice. She tried to temper the hope in her own voice with a reserved patience.

"That's the thing. They did," Kerri stated firmly. She continued more cautiously, "But the caller, a preacher, said a woman came in to the church and asked them if they could track down what happened to some babies she'd dropped off at a meeting that took place there."

"Why would she go there and not to the hospital?"

Kerri had already written that question down on her pad. She ticked it when DD said it, silently agreeing that something was not right. Kerri tapped her pencil eraser on the pad, thinking of how to relay the situation as clearly as possible.

"That was the pastor's first question. Once he tracked down the people from the meeting, they told him that the woman said she didn't want attention to her, so she found an after-hours meeting of mothers," Kerri said with a note of disbelief. "Just *gave* them to someone."

"So… nowhere, still? Or did he find that mother?" Doug David asked, the panic evident in her voice.

Kerri tried to project confidence over the phone line. She looked at her tablet and briskly began going down the list of what she did for DD to process. "I called the group leader, who said the person who took the babies hadn't been to a meeting in a long time. Didn't answer her phone. Then I called the hospital. After I got forwarded about ten times, I had a very interesting talk with a long-time employee there who I have known for a while. He and I go way back; that may be the only reason he told me anything," Kerri admitted. "Anyway, this guy said he did, in fact, remember the babies being brought in for a checkup. He'd been part of the disposition of the case."

"What does that mean? Disposal means they're dead?" DD yelled into Kerri's ear.

"No, no. It just means what they did about it," Kerri soothed. "Apparently, they didn't follow each and every rule exactly with them. He got cagey with me about it, near the end. Asked me did I have a Kansas case number."

Daring to hope, Doug David said, "What does all that mean?"

"Well, that's what I was going to tell you. If he's asking about a case number, it means he is already thinking about the legal situation. The legality of what he did and what the group did and what whoever might have the babies did," Kerri assessed. "It means, first, don't get your hopes up, but it also means this is more than we've ever found out. It also means, in my opinion, those babies are down there and findable. So, yes. I'm going to continue to investigate. I will definitely call you every time I get a new scrap of information. OK, Doug David?"

Kerri said the last bit as soft and as tender as Doug David ever remembered a person speaking to her. "May the Lord have Mercy. Thank you," she replied as tears swelled in her eyes.

Kerri heard the beginnings of a sob before DD hung up the phone. She understood completely.

Kerri put her head in her hands, allowing hope to wash over her, fully and completely.

Kerri's investigation and discovery of what had taken place in Enid on the date in question over a year ago could have been lifted out of a textbook; the lesson about determination in the face of very few facts. She had a date to ask about, and two babies left with no one in attendance. She found the names of the charge nurses on duty during that timeframe from the scheduler at the hospital, when her contact forwarded the call. Many of the staff had moved on, as medical staff tends to do, but she finally spoke with the very same nurse who met the caregiver mother and initiated the care for the babies.

Kerri read reports indicating that both children were undernourished, that they had irritated stomachs and throats, and that one of them showed signs of thrush. After running the two through the standard tests they give every newborn, and giving them the standard raft of immunizations and protections, including the vitamin K greasy paste they put on every baby's eyelids, the pediatric resident declared them fit and healthy. They were much happier with actual formula to drink and started to gurgle and smile, especially when they pooped.

Kerri found out that the sketchy stuff happened as soon as the administrative staff said the children could continue staying with the new caregiver and then, possibly, be adopted. The minutes from a meeting were clear on that. But the next meeting's minutes, from two weeks later, only said the case of the two babies had been handled satisfactorily and that a local charity had taken the lead and the hospital considered the matter closed. The name of the charity was not listed in the minutes, though Kerri suspected a redaction, and Kerri's equivalent case officer in Enid had no notice or information concerning pending foster care and adoption.

At that point, the trail had run cold. Had Kerri not cared as much as she did, she wouldn't have gotten a phone book out and called each and every charity in the Enid yellow pages. She called every food pantry. She called every soup kitchen. Asked the same few questions. Her last call—the definitive call—went to a small, home-based charity with only a phone number and a P.O. Box listed in the phone book, called "The Lamb's Buggy." A woman answered on the fifth ring.

"Hello? Lambs," said the woman.

"Hi, is this The Lamb's Buggy?" Kerri asked.

"Uh. Yes, it is. I'd forgotten this number rang here, but yes, this is it."

Kerri paused, hearing toddlers in the background, before saying, "My name is Kerri, and I work for Child Services in Kansas. I'm looking for two babies who were left at an Enid Municipal Hospital fourteen months ago. Do you know anything about that?"

Kerri heard a child's brief cry in the background.

"Don't call here again. I don't know anything about that," the woman said, abruptly cutting off the call.

"I sat at my desk for a good five minutes, Doug David," Kerri said when she called her, "because I knew those were your babies. I don't know all the details, but she had your kids. And I was going to get to the bottom of it."

Doug David couldn't speak, but she couldn't bear to hang up either. In the end, she handed the phone to Mac, who listened to Kerri, took a few notes in his scrawling rancher's hand, and said "thank you" over and over.

Another month of legal wrangling ensued, with the competing state offices of child welfare claiming both jurisdiction and a lack of the same, before a plan of action was in place, approved by both halves of the system. After the departments agreed, Kerri called DD to advise her that a meeting would happen between two social workers, the "foster mother"—as they were calling her—and DD.

Every day seemed endless as DD waited for the imminent meeting between herself and the other woman. The woman who had taken two babies out of a church meeting and claimed them for her own. Both social workers agreed that Kerri would meet Doug David at the foster mother's house, but even getting that intermediary step solidified was exhausting. Mac would drive DD down there and Kerri would take her own car.

CHAPTER TWENTY-FIVE

Doug David, weary from the two-hour drive (the longest she'd ever ridden by far), stepped out of passenger side of the old Ford Taurus Mac drove, and stood on the curb with the car between her and the playground surrounded with a wrought-iron fence. Mac stretched and tipped his cap back on his head. Kerri had already been parked when they got there, and another official-looking woman stepped out of a sedan when Mac pulled up. They shook hands all around. The Oklahoma social worker, whose name DD immediately forgot, said she'd had the opportunity to meet the foster mother and was comfortable staying outside, at least initially, while DD met her.

Kerri agreed to the same thing, but said, "All you have to do is come out on the porch and get us, DD. We are all here for the same thing. We want everyone safe and sound, right?"

"I'll just stay out here, too, DD," Mac added quietly. "You go on up to the door. Come back out if you need me, okay?"

The day before, after Kerri called, DD found Mac in the barn and asked him if he minded driving her down there in the sedan in the morning.

"I'm scared stiff, Mac," DD had admitted.

"Now don't you worry; hardest part is over. I wouldn't miss going down there for all the world, DD," he said. "I'll just make sure she starts and give 'er a once over."

Now, DD took a few hesitant steps towards the house, then set her shoulders and walked right up to the door and knocked. No one answered right away. She kept knocking. She didn't see or hear the girls in the side yard anymore. She knocked one more time and then the door opened slowly.

A woman answered the door, wary. "I wondered how long it would take for you to get here. Can I help you?" she asked.

"My name is Doug David. I think your two kids are my babies," she said. "I have nothing. I don't even own that car, let alone a house," Doug David said to the woman. "I would never ask you this if there was any other way."

The young foster mother, face wearied by burdens unknown, held the door open and invited her in. "My name is Janice," she finally said. "Janice Lamb. I've heard the social worker's version and, forgive me if I sound skeptical, but could you explain your side of it?"

DD stepped through the door, waited until the woman motioned to the two chairs with a table and lamp in between them. The carpet was a dark brown shag, and all of the furnishings looked like thrift store finds. DD told the woman a shortened summary of her life; her parents then Alaine then how it all unwound. How everyone had dispersed, including her babies, and their waning hopes of reunion hinging on Kerri, the social worker.

"That, then, is how I got here," DD concluded. "I got pregnant by a young man named Trout, who lived on the farm with me and many others. We didn't know what we were getting into when we fell in love. It's not like we didn't know how babies were made, but it just seemed like it wouldn't happen to us because we were the children on the farm."

"How old were you?" the woman asked.

"I'm pretty sure I was 16, and he was either 17 or 18. Birthdays weren't a big deal; my mom could hardly bear to celebrate mine."

"Why is that?" she asked with skepticism.

"Well, that, and the story of my name, are a tale for another time, if you don't mind," Doug David said. "I have a few questions of my own."

"I thought you might."

"First of all, I have to say thank you. Who knows what would have happened if you hadn't taken them," she said, holding her hand up to stop the woman from speaking. "But that's the nicest thing you'll hear in the next few minutes."

The woman's face closed; her eyes turned wary.

"My main question is this: how dare you cheat your way into taking babies, *anyone's* babies? What did you have to tell yourself to make that kind of horrible behavior acceptable?"

The woman sat silent for a long time. Minutes. Minutes are an eternity when there is nothing else to do except wait for an explanation that makes sense.

"I used to be married. My husband left me. He loved someone else. He didn't even tell me in person. He called me. And had papers sent over within a week. He'd clearly been planning to leave for a while. He didn't want anything in the house. He didn't want to see me. He said this other woman was going to have his child, because I couldn't."

Doug David had committed to listen to her, whatever she had to say, but, on the way up the porch steps, had told herself to demand her babies back and not take no for an answer.

"We'd tried for years. We lived on the Gulf coast for a while. It was wonderful. He came from a big family and couldn't wait to get started on ours. I just kept having my period. It hurt him more than I suffered from it. His mother tried to get me to take a whole bunch of supplements, his father said I needed to be in church more. It got so the family was *angry* at me. *Blamed* me. For not getting pregnant."

Doug David sat in a steely, tearless silence, resolved to make this woman admit that she stole her children. Tried to continue to see her as a narrator, removed from the story. But at the laying of blame that Janice spoke of, she began to see a thread of similarity. She listened, curious now. "I know a little something about misguided holy directions," Doug David allowed. "Why is it that men are never wrong?"

Janice indicated her agreement with a sigh and tilt of the head. "I convinced him that we needed a fresh start. Away from his family, which, I told him, was corroding me. My hair was falling out, I said. It wasn't, but he'd stopped noticing by then. We moved here where there was another oil job for him, and I could take walks in the country and volunteer in the hospital." She smiled wearily. "I thought maybe being around babies would encourage my womb to freshen and get the hint."

Janice shrugged her shoulders and raised her hands, palms up. "Of course that didn't work. I had it checked out one time after a volunteer shift. I mean, I made an appointment and the whole thing. I didn't tell my husband; he'd already given up. They told me, in a bunch of medical jargon, that it was *extremely* unlikely that I would ever be able to 'be impregnated.'

That's the phrase they used; not even a warm feeling to go along with the cold news."

Janice took a drink. She'd had a glass of clear liquid with her when Doug David came to the door. She still hadn't offered to get anything for Doug David, not that she would be able to drink or eat anything, anyway.

"They told me a three percent chance. A three percent chance of rain, you still go to the park to play, right? Crushing news. My hopes—well, I guess they were gone with that. So, I started a daycare. Better than nothing. I watched a few of the nurse's kids while they worked. It was easy and fun and helped them out, too. I barely charged them any money. We didn't need it. And, if I really tried to earn money— ever—my husband just laughed and asked me 'what skills are you planning on selling?' and stuff like that. Then the babies showed up at that meeting."

"You were there? When they showed up?" Doug David remembered what Kerri had told her about the meeting of already-mothers and hopeful-mothers and mothers-of-loss. She marveled at that; how so many could be taken in by the story Rosie told about rescue and the need for secrecy.

"Yep. I always went. I just wanted to listen to mothers talk about babies. Baby crazy, I guess," she said with a rueful chuckle. "After I volunteered to take them, I called one of my few friends at foster care, asked her what I needed to do to qualify. She said she'd bring the papers over that afternoon, and she'd take care of making sure I met the requirements, backdate a few things, if necessary. Those babies went home with me and I immediately just… claimed them. My heart did, anyway."

Doug David was incredulous. "So… they just let you keep them? No one asked about them ever, or came to check on them?" She tried to keep the shock out of her voice when she asked.

Janice saw the look on her face, though, and grimaced. "Oh, my friend at the foster agency did, sure," she admitted. "She called me now and then. Made sure I was taking care of them. She said she 'buried the paperwork' and that no one would bother me about it. Said it was 'her gift' to me because she knew how sad I was about not having my own children."

Another pause. More silence. The edge of distrust had left the room, and a sense of the vastness of a mother's love had invaded both of them, in spite of their opposing positions.

"May I use your bathroom, please?" Doug David asked.

Janice stood, motioned down the hall. "Certainly, of course," she said, a hint of desperation raising the pitch of her voice.

Doug David wandered down the hallway, looking closely at the pictures that lined both walls. Little babies in matching outfits, then just-walking babies, then toddlers, still in matching clothes, posed on playground equipment, fields of wheat, and Santa's sleigh.

She used the bathroom then walked farther down the hall, seeing the two doors at the end of the hallway. One led to a master bedroom where the blankets on the king-sized bed were messily turned down on only one side of the bed. The other door was pulled almost shut, but not latched.

Doug David heard a gentle whimper through the crack in the door. Pushed it open barely an inch. Breathed in and out. Looked in and saw two cribs, at right angles to each other. One child stood in a crib, squatting up and down. The other child slept on, not bothered by the sound of the first.

DD slumped against the door; she'd never been this close to her children, at least not when she was healthy, alert, and conscious enough to realize it. The roomful of scents that surround motherhood rushed her right back to the bedroom on the farm where she'd lain for the last portion of the pregnancy. The place that Alaine insisted was *all she needed for the Lord to deliver the Next Generation of Believers.*

"Would you like to go in? See them?" Janice asked, suddenly standing behind her in the hallway.

Doug David had not registered Janice's approach. She nodded, "I'd like that very much."

A tear, then two, then a rush of them as she stepped into the presence of her tiny (now not so tiny), perfect creations. She went to the sleeping baby first, just to look. She took in the blonde hair of the baby, piled next to her, some of it winding around her neck. Thought of her mother's hair; her own hair when she was young. "What have you named this one?" Doug David asked.

"That's Grace," Janice said. "This one is Ellie, for Eleison."

"That reminds me of the Bible. For mercy," Doug David said. "We studied it, just in case the Lord came back speaking Greek."

Janice first smiled, thinking that she was making a joke; realized she was sincere before any damage was done. "Exactly the word I was thinking of. Her foster records say Eleison, but I've always called her Ellie."

Ellie, the one who had been awake when Doug David peeked in, stretched her arms out to Janice, mewing quietly to be picked up, held, loved. Doug David watched that happen, wondering if her heart had already permanently broken, and that's why she didn't ache, or that little Ellie had only ever known Janice, so of course she'd want her.

Janice picked up Ellie and held her, looking at Doug David with chagrin. Maybe regret. "Listen. Doug David, I never thought this would hurt anyone. I had no idea, the woman who dropped them off said she would call when it was safe!"

"Yeah. Apparently, the woman who took the babies never intended to keep them. Left them with you. Had a change of heart and called the church. Before that, I had one single person in Kansas looking. One."

Grace, the sleeping baby, stirred, rolled over, looked at the two women. Looked at her sister in Janice's arms, made the same beseeching mewing sounds to be held. Doug David looked at Janice.

"May I?"

Janice smiled in answer. Watched Doug David lift Grace from the crib, pull her close and hold her so she could see both Janice and Ellie. This seemed to satisfy Grace, and she reached a hand out to lightly tap Ellie on the face. They smiled at each other. Doug David buried her face in Grace's hair, breathing in. Breathing out, her eyes closed.

"Would you like to help me feed them?" Janice asked.

Doug David knew then that her heart had not, in fact, shut down, because it broke anew with this peace offering from Janice. She turned and followed her out to the kitchen, where Grace and Ellie each had a high chair. Janice got food, spoons, juice, crackers out and set them close. She told Doug David to sit next to Ellie, and Janice sat by Grace.

"Just use small spoonfuls at first," Janice instructed. "They always eat slowly right when they wake up. Put a few crackers on the tray. They pick them up when they are done with the jarred food. They drink from their sippy cups themselves, and they'll get mad if you try to help them. It's adorable."

Doug David explored this strange, delightful, foreign world with fascination. Her heart leapt every time Ellie took a bite. Doug David studied the finger painting of food left on the tray, searching it for deeper meaning. She laughed in spite of herself. "I've fed baby animals before. Back on the farm. But this—this is a whole new wonderful," she said.

"It is. These two are the only thing that kept me alive the last two years," Janice confessed. "I'm not saying that to make you feel bad. I'm serious; I'd have shut it all down if I hadn't had them."

"Shut it all down?"

"I think pills is the way I would have gone."

"Pills?"

Janice stopped feeding Grace, looked at Doug David full on with a quizzical look on her face. "Do you seriously not understand that I would have taken my own life—stopped living—if these two wouldn't have come to be my children?"

Doug David, having lived in a protected place—even if it was a twisted protection—hadn't understood that was a real option to a person unhappy with their existence. "I'm sorry. I didn't realize that. I'm still not very good at normal life."

"Where do you live now?" Janice asked.

"I live on a farm. A different farm. With a man named Mac. I mean, not *with* him, like his woman, but more as a permanent guest. I guess," she said. "I didn't have any other relatives or anything."

"Is it nice? Is it—" Janice gestured helplessly. "I don't know… hopeful?"

"Well, I think, after all this time pining away, I think it's one of the few places where I could have been to keep thinking there was a chance at finding them."

"What do you do to fill your days up?"

"Mac has cows. Milk cows and beef cattle. I help him with that. I get the eggs. I plant and harvest the garden. Farm stuff. Like I used to do. He's got this great pond with all kinds of fish in it; I go throw a line in there now and then. Have you ever fished?"

"Oh my god!—gosh!" she checked her language at a look from Doug David. "We went out on the Gulf in a boat. My husband always wanted to catch those huge bonito fish or a swordfish. Ridiculous; I was seasick each and every time!"

"I've been in a canoe. That's it, though. I've never seen the ocean."

Grace and Ellie were done eating, and had started banging the crackers into little crumbs on their trays. Had started asking to get down. Janice stood up to get a washcloth. She got two and ran warm water over both of them. Wrung them out. Handed one to Doug David.

"If you'll just take the tray off first, then they stay clean better," Janice said.

"Makes sense." Doug David reached out for Ellie with the cloth. "Here, little one, let me wipe your hands off before you get down." She didn't realize she'd used the same language her mother had, back when Doug David was a child.

Ellie was scrabbling at the restraining belt that held her in place, tugging at it with decreasing patience and increasing fierceness. Doug David quickly finished the cleaning, undid the belt, and lifted her out then down from the high chair.

"She's got a stubborn streak, that's for sure," Janice laughed. "They like to go read books after they eat. Come on."

Doug David trailed after the three, absorbing the joy of the routine, the simple pleasure at giving love to a tiny human. They all returned to the front living room, where the pile of books was immediately toppled and spread across the floor, so the girls could see each title available. Finally, a picture book selected, Grace held it up to Janice, who took it, and both girls climbed up on the couch, where Doug David sat next to Janice.

"Here," Janice said, handing over the book. "You read it. I've read this one a thousand times to them. They want this one every day."

Doug David took the book, felt the perfect bundles of heat and trust that nestled on either side of her, wept some more tears, and began to read.

CHAPTER TWENTY-SIX

A knock on the door came during the fourth book in the session. Janice looked startled. Doug David stopped reading. They both turned to the door. A woman was peering through the glass, trying to see in. Mac stood right next to her, looking uncomfortable.

"The social worker," Janice said. "I forgot she was here. But who is that man?"

"That's Mac. It's his farm I live on. What does this lady want?" Doug David asked.

Janice swept the door open, inviting them both inside. The woman had a concerned look on her face, and gripped her faux-leather portfolio tightly.

"Please. Come in!" Janice said with a chirp.

"Janice, are you OK?" the woman asked loudly. "I've been worried out here, not sure if I should interrupt."

"DD, this is Ms. Walker," Janice said. "She's handling the case, at least as far as Oklahoma goes." She turned to the social worker. "Ms. Walker, I'm so sorry! It's all my fault. We are fine. All four of us are fine."

DD had met Ms. Walker before she knocked on Janice's door, but so much had happened that it was a new meeting. DD smiled at her, hesitantly, and stepped closer to Janice.

Ms. Walker's face relaxed a tiny bit when she said, "Truly? Are you all ok? I'd never forgive myself if something happened. It was an odd arrangement to not immediately remove the children, and then when I realized after talking with Kerri and Mr. Tillman here that you are the birth mother and might have plans we haven't processed—"

"No, it's ok," Janice assured her. "Turns out it's best we got a chance to talk with no backup, I guess." She waved toward the sofa. "Come sit down. The little girls are just playing and throwing books. It's one of their favorite things to do. We can talk," she smiled, "and you can see for yourself."

Mac motioned he would stay on the porch, already seating himself on the rocker and stretching his legs out. Kerri stood out there and indicated she'd stay outside, too.

"Thank you," Ms. Walker said. "And, I'm so relieved! These things don't always go well."

Doug David looked at her, then at Janice, then rested her face on the two little ones. Her smiled beamed, and her cheeks had a glow to them that was more than just the recent cleansing they'd had by tears. "It's been wonderful. I can't even tell you. I'm so thankful to have found them."

Janice looked a little desperate when she heard that, but didn't say anything.

Ms. Walker looked down at the portfolio open on her lap. "Well, the first thing we need to do is establish custody and guardianship of the children. We've got to fill out these forms for relocation, then we've got to establish the penalty and the damages. Lastly, we need to decide what we will file with the court, and which state court we will file in."

At that recitation, Doug David looked with alarm at Janice, whose face had filled with fear and grief. An understanding passed between them, almost faster than thought.

Doug David reached a hand out to stop Ms. Walker's speech. "Excuse me, Ms. Walker, could you give us one second? Just watch these two while we go talk? We'll be quick about it."

"I—that would be fine," Ms. Walker said. She looked doubtfully at the two children playing at her feet.

"We'll just be in the kitchen, ma'am," Janice told her.

The two women—one the birth mother, one the caregiving mother—scurried into the kitchen. They huddled together while Janice turned the water on in the sink.

Doug David spoke first, "I don't want *any* of that. None of it."

"Me *neither*. I don't know what to do!"

"The problem, for you, anyway, is that you never adopted them. They're just in foster care, right?"

"Yes. I guess that's true."

"But what if—"

"That means you legally get them, doesn't it?" Janice finally realizing.

"But what if this?" Doug David started again.

"You have all the say? How can that be just?" Janice had started to cry, her voice rising in despair. "I have to do what you say! I don't even get to give my side of the story. Or anything! Please don't take my babies away today!"

"Janice! Listen to me. I have an idea. But you've got to be quiet so Ms. Walker won't hear us; I don't think she'd like us making our own rules."

"I'll try," she sniffled.

"What if," Doug David tried a third time, "you moved? What if you'd had enough of this house—you hate it, right?—I took the babies, and you just *happened* to move to a farm in Kansas?"

"You'll take them?" she cried. "I knew you would! It's my worst fear."

"No, listen," DD said in an urgent murmur. "Yes, I'll take them. *But...* what if I hired someone to help me raise my two babies? I'm still a teenager, after all. What if I just *happened* to hire you to be a live-in caregiver?"

"You'd be their mother? And all I would be is the babysitter?" Janice moaned.

"We'd *both* be their mothers!" Doug David was bursting with glee, elated by the idea. "It's perfect; all we have to do is fill out the papers, thank her, go our separate ways. You could come back with me this very second, or, better yet, I could say I need a week or two to get my living situation under control so I could care for them properly. Kerri is brilliant at that kind of thing; I'm sure of it! Then you come up. Mac would *love* to have babies running around."

She grabbed Janice's hands. Looked her in the face, pulled her close in a hug. Janice, after a second, hugged her back, tighter and tighter.

CHAPTER TWENTY-SEVEN

The plan, in short, worked. Both the Oklahoma and Kansas departments of child services had enough signed paperwork to be satisfied, and even a presiding custody judge in each state gave the arrangement a cursory study, approving the official relocation of the two babies to the birth mother. Neither department nor judge was further interested in the real estate sale of the home in Oklahoma, the moving of a single woman to a neighboring state, or the subsequent rental of a room in a farmhouse in rural Sedgwick County by that same single woman.

Mac had taken about ten seconds to be convinced that Doug David's plan was worth a try. As soon as he heard the joy in her voice he was ready to accede to whatever she asked. It was little enough sacrifice to clear out two of the vacant, dusty bedrooms for both Janice and the little ones.

Doug David was a whirling dervish during the week before Janice and the girls moved up to join them. She cleaned, she dusted, she even stripped and repainted the window frames "just in case they still had lead paint in them." Which he was sure they didn't, or he would have insisted she use a mask and follow the protective guidelines. It was easier, and more enjoyable, to just let her tear around and get the living space ready. He was gratified and a little touched that one girl was named Grace, and the other's name meant mercy.

It was exactly what all of them needed. He could feel his Jules smiling down upon his new family.

Doug David read the headline of the newspaper with the barest of interest. "Cult Leader's Sons Imprisoned for Life after Jury's Decision" it exclaimed above the fold in huge black letters.

"Did you see this, Mac?" she asked, showing him the paper.

"I did see that. I guess they finally found them once they knew who they should be looking for."

"Is that the boys?" Janice inquired. "The ones who lived on your farm?"

"Yep. Well, one of them is Trout," Doug David replied. "The father of our two. The other is his brother, Pike, who I'm sure was the trouble behind them following everything Alaine told them to do."

DD and Janice spoke of the children with a shared parenthood, free from ego or possession. They trusted each other to do right for the girls, no matter what.

"Are you sad?" asked Janice, reaching for DD's hand.

Doug David sat and wondered about that. She thought back to loving Trout. The days of spring where they chased each other with an endless appetite, spiced by the danger of avoiding the rules. The now-obviously twisted rules designed to keep the kids corralled and under the constant disapproving eye of all the adults, even if they only reported to Alaine. She still could not believe anyone had been taken in by Alaine's increasingly paranoid and heavy-handed leadership. That it took Rosie stealing her children; her father and mother trying to escape and get help to tear the straitjacket of restrictive fabric apart for the rest of them. That it had vanished like so much smoke on the wind. She marvelled at her new life empty of parents but full of those she loved as new family.

DD looked at Janice, then Mac, with a weary smile. "I'm not sad, no. It would never have worked. Not out here in the real world. Both those boys were entitled brats, poisoned by their father's—I guess he wasn't their real father—Alaine's abusive worldview. That he, and by extension they, deserved everything they wanted, whether right or not."

Mac and Janice looked at each other, a peace on each face, watching Doug David's internal replay.

They heard the door handle rattle at the same time from the kids' room, and they both stood up.

"The girls are up. Mac and I will go get them," Janice said. "Be right back."

ACKNOWLEDGEMENTS

Though writing is a solitary business, I'd still be stuck writing first drafts without the help and support I've received along the way from a great many people and organizations. The Kansas/Missouri Chapter of the Society of Children's Book Writers and Illustrators (SCBWI) hosts a Writing Retreat at a monastery in Missouri, where I spent several weekends working on my writing. Way-Word Writers—started by my friends and colleagues Heather, Stephanie, and Nicki—hosted a Writing Retreat in Branson, and the opportunity to be in contact with many accomplished authors was trajectory-changing for my writing. I will always remember the evenings when we read our work aloud for the sheer joy of hearing each other's creativity. The Kansas Writers Association is a very supportive group that meets monthly in Wichita, and I am grateful for their positivity and expertise.

Harvester Arts in Wichita invited me to their 2024 Artist INC cohort; I'll be forever grateful for the opportunity they gave me. (And I still feel like I got lucky with all the talent I was able to work with there!) They work hand in hand with Mid-America Arts Alliance (M-AAA), supporting artists at all stages of creativity in a six-state area. David Wayne Reed of M-AAA gave me career-changing advice in our Artist

INC post-cohort collaboration meeting—thank you for your zeal, belief, and suggestions on my work.

My thanks to Scott Walker, my editor found through Reedsy.com. Your time, attention, and focus on my story made it much better. The beautiful cover art is by my friend and colleague Lindsey Kernodle. Thanks to Londyn at LC Photography for the headshot session. To my friend and fellow writer, Leslie—I had no idea that pike are an aggressive and mean fish; your insight into the character Pike helped me make him a worse version of himself, which in turn made DD's escape all the more precarious.

It takes dozens of people spending time in conversation with me for these characters to emerge and insist that I tell their story for them. To all those I've bounced ideas off for the past few years... thank you for listening.

Angie, you're my always and forever partner and friend and love. I can't wait for our next chapter.

Please standby for DD, Grace, and Ellie as they grow and make the world a better place. That story is coming, and it will bring a lot of joy.